THE COMPANION

THE COMPANION
Laurence Staig

To Debbie
With Best Wishes

Laurence Staig

THE BROOLIGAN PRESS
LONDON
NEW YORK

First published as Shapeshifter in 1992 by Lions, an imprint of Harper Collins Publishers Ltd

This revised edition published 2018 by The Broolligan Press

ISBN-13: 978 1 9999207 7 7

For Susan Dickinson, who suspended disbelief

AUTHOR'S NOTE

When I was 10, due to their business commitments, my parents decided to send me to a Boarding School one summer. The school was in Eastbourne, not far from Beachy Head. It was gothic in appearance, with straggling ivy everywhere. I didn't care for the place, it was a far cry from Brixton in South London where I lived and I only lasted a term. However, it was here that I was introduced to a collection of ghost stories entitled *Ghost Stories of An Antiquary*, by another, slightly older boy. The collection was of course written by one of the greatest ever ghost story writers—M R James. From the moment that I read the first story, *Canon Alberic's Scrapbook*, I was hooked, and have been a devotee ever since.

This novel is my tribute to James, and I won't have been the first, (or the last) writer to acknowledge a debt to a story teller many regard as the master. I have deliberately used many Jamesian references, those who know his stories might be quick to catch them.

The Companion was originally published by HarperCollins in 1992 as *Shapeshifter* and marketed at the 'Young Adult' audience. 'Young Adult' has always been a term I have felt uncomfortable with. A good story should be just that: a good story. *The Companion* is not targeted at any particular age range and this new and revised version (I hope) defies categorising. I simply aimed to write a ghost story that would give the reader a genuinely unnerving experience. I am grateful to The Brooligan Press for the opportunity for the resurrection.

Laurence Staig
Honington, Suffolk 2018

She looked out of the window as white as any milk
And he looked in at the window as black as any silk.

She became a corpse, a corpse all in the ground
And he became the cold clay and smothered her all
    around.

The Two Magicians
Trad. English Folk Song

PRELUDE FROM ANOTHER TIME

"TURN, TURN pretty one. That's my lovely, that's my treasure. First this way and then that. Oh, what delight, with what gladness you fill my heart. Can you dance? Just a step perhaps, maybe if I clap my hands like this, you will find it easier? Or perhaps, like this?

Oh, too fast, too fast, my poor boy, my dear, to make you gad and tumble there, in such an ungainly fashion, so, so, unfair. Steady now. Twirl, twirl, that's the way my pretty, that's the way.

What's that you say? You're tired?

No matter.

Hist whist!

Up now, on your pretty toes, to make you taller, to make your swan neck grow. Raise your chin a little more. Such a pretty neck, your finest feature I should say. Up my dear. Now turn a little to the right, now twist to the left, the light, my child, my child, mind the light—this is your better side. Trust me. Young fool, where is your sense? Have you no soul?

Now turn.

Do as I say, please.

Do it.

Stretch up, the chin. Now hold. Hold as I say. Just there. That's it. Oh, I grow giddy from your beauty.

Now listen, very carefully. Don't move. Not a single muscle.

Can you hear your heart beat, my dear? Such a heart. I can see the tiny pulse in your neck, just there, beckoning to me almost. Be still. Young fool!

Not a jot. Damn you, damn your soul be still or be cursed!

Still!—Don't make me rage, I warn you now.

Better.

Curse your eyes. Be as still as bones in a grave, as silent as a shroud. Hear me well, if I so much as see the air stir before your pretty lips, you'll never take breath again.

Ahhh!

That's better.

Much better.

Now I can watch you.

Good.

Weary? Oh my dear, there will be rest.

Not now though, no—not now.

Let me just watch you, direct you, we'll soon have your fine form captured here by my friend.

Stand as you are, there are many more hours till morning, aren't there my lovely?

Aren't there?

Let the capture commence."

ONE

ABOVE THEM, the sky bled: the light diffusing slowly through the clouds with a deepening orange glow. Two of the 'imps', tumbled out from the back of the old camper van. Their excited arms waved like empty sleeves as they tangled with one another's spindly jean-clad legs. They were clambering, shuffling for the honour to be the first to set foot on the soil of the summer place.

Sprog, being the smallest, had a natural talent for easing and squeezing herself through the most awkward and impossible of gaps. She slid herself beneath Bella's legs, falling down onto the grass with the ease of a dropped calf.

Throwing her head back she laughed with triumph. The gap in her teeth made her appear more mischievous than usual. She could have been a creature from fairy land.

"Me, me, me! It's me. Touch earth first! Touch earth first!" The cry could have been a spell.

Bella came next, but with more dignity.

"Touch earth second," she said, quietly.

Pippa, the eldest of the trio, remained framed within the opening of the van. Her hands rested on the sides. For a moment, she became transformed into a wild creature, with ragged button-bib dungarees. Her strawberry blonde hair burned flame red. The colour was richer than usual: it was the effect of the evening light. For a moment the two sisters stopped laughing and looked up at her.

Pippa had frozen.

Bella caught Pippa's moment of silence: it was

7

unnatural. The light made her into a shape without substance, her features a haze.

"What's wrong, Pippa?" asked Bella.

"Nothing," came a short reply.

Bella twisted her head round. Pippa had been looking out past where they lay, captured by something far more interesting than their antics. Bella didn't believe Pippa's explanation for her abruptness. Something else had caused her mood change.

Then Bella saw it too: the Grange.

Bathed in gleaming twilight, the building melted effortlessly into the evening sky. The setting might have been stolen from the canvas of a painting. Images were still, stiff-frozen where they stood like captured dreams.

Bella held her breath and pulled herself round onto her haunches, into a more comfortable sitting position. Sprog still lay on her back staring at the sky. She was watching small bats fly past overhead, screeching with tiny toy-like voices as they passed. Thinking that they were birds, she wondered why they sounded so strange.

Bella now realized the true reason for Pippa's still moment. Their father had sent them a photograph a few weeks previously, taken in bright sunlight. It showed him on the steps of the house in his leather apron and with a length of lead in one hand. It had been a picture of Dad rather than the Grange, although the house was the reason he had sent it. Now she was looking at the place itself for the first time, set in a frame of tall trees.

They stared together, picking up on detail as though they might have been building surveyors.

The roof was a staggered mix of spires, conical shapes and sloping slates that stopped abruptly at ridges. It was like architectural geometry. From the ridges smaller roofs became interestingly shaped gables, with acutely angled peaks, displaying a perfect symmetry. The windows stretched upwards, with long and slender pointed gable roofs that looked like hats. Some of them had green and amber ivy for hair, that fell from either side of the eaves.

A stretch of perfectly flat lawn, heralded the approach to the stone-stepped entrance. Hedges bordered the frontage on either side. There was a low wall of flint and brick at the front, typical of Suffolk, topped by square stone sections with decorative orbs. Before this splendor there was the huge pond, this was the most arresting feature of the view. The house was reflected with a mirror-like precision in the water; it could have been a twin, but the reflection basked in an orange sheen. The surface of the water shone, pitted only occasionally by a floating piece of bark, set there as if in aspic.

Sprog had, by now, also sat up. The bats had gone away, disappearing in a series of loops and circles, and the silence puzzled her. She copied her sister and half closed her eyes.

A stillness hung on the air, heavy and mysterious. For just a moment Sprog thought she saw something raise its head above the water. A series of dark rings stained the surface as the animal disappeared.

"It's magic," said Sprog seriously, suddenly feeling as if she should contribute a comment.

"Let's help Dad unload," said Pippa, changing the subject.

Sprog continued to watch the pond, a grin slowly spreading across her face.

"Are there any frogs in there?" She asked.

"Let's just unload," repeated Pippa firmly.

"Think that'd suit him fine," said a voice from somewhere around the side of the camper van. A tall man, craggy-faced with sunken cheeks, and with a bunched peaked cap, appeared. This was Bob Ford, the man who had met their father as they had driven into the village.

He continued. "Problem is we ain't quite there yet, not quite. There's a road that leads round the back. Your pa tol' me he wanted you to see this, not jus' from the car neither, that's why we've all got out here. S'pose it's the most interesting view you'll have of the house, dunno it's worth a stop, though."

He paused as if reconsidering his last comment.

"Startlin', ain't it?" he added.

"It's beautiful," Bella decided. "Everything shines, everything, even the trees."

Bob Ford shuffled forwards with a cigarette paper held between his fingers. He was arranging strands of woolly tobacco along its length, a match carefully seating the strands into place.

"You could say she shines, I s'pose."

Bella blinked hard, to clear her eyes. Darkly delineated edges appeared firm and proud against the sky one minute, and yet when she took a second glance, images blurred with a strange shining glow. There was an awful seriousness here too. Even Bob Ford who seemed friendly at first, now looked severe, his bushy eyebrows had become thicker, and his jowls harder.

"She's an old place, mostly fall'n down. Looks all right from the outside, I s'pose. It's dark inside, though. Dark and damp in the long nights. Let's hope the summer's good, and your pa finishes up 'fore winter. Best outa there in the winter. Whole damn house should've gone down years ago, really. Nobody aroun' here wants it."

"Is Dad's church near here?" asked Sprog, jumping to her feet. She ran over to where Bob Ford stood.

She looked up with angel eyes, her mouth hung open, displaying her gap-toothed grin again. Bob Ford had thought she was a boy when he had first met her.

"Not far, my ol' love," Bob Ford laughed without there being any humour. "It's through that clump of trees, to the right there. You'll see it later, soon enough, soon enough."

"This is where we're staying, Sprog," Bella explained, as she caught Sprog's hand and led her to the front of the camper van. "The church is in that little wood, where Mr Ford said. You can just see the sunset sparkling in the windows—there through the trees."

Sprog could see nothing in the church windows. For her there were only fleeting glimmers of light, which chased through the trees, like the dart of moonrise sprites.

Kit Farris, the 'Imps' father, had already climbed out of the driver's seat and walked towards the edge of the pond. He was gazing across to the Grange with a lost and distant expression.

Pippa joined him, linking her arm with his. He was a tall man, but she was already the height of his shoulder. For a moment, she watched with him. His greying beard became hard-edged in the twilight, the steel of his eyes wise and assuring, yet there was something that clearly bothered him. He made a strange sound with his teeth.

"It's not all ours," he said without turning, his voice sounded flat. "I mean, to live in that is. Most of it has fallen into ruin. The secretary from the diocese office told me that one family closed up each room as more plaster fell off the ceiling. Then they simply moved on into another room. They left eventually, doing a moonlight flit. Can't say I blame them, really.

"We've got the rooms off the central hall and a couple upstairs. It's clean. We've got electric, and a land-line phone that works when it wants to."

He sighed and looked tense.

"I caught it once like this before, recently, coming back late from the church. I came through over there through the trees. I'd taken out a nave window. I thought the problem was with me, that I had been working too close to the glass. I couldn't make my mind up if it was beautiful or . . . or whether . . ." He became unsure of what words he should use. "I saw something else too, you see." He licked his lip.

Pippa remained silent, her father didn't usually talk this way.

"We should be gettin' on, Mr Farris," said Bob Ford, suddenly.

Without turning, Farris nodded and squeezed his daughter's arm. She pulled him away, her gaze lingering for a few moments over the view as she did so. Before she made her way back to the camper van, it struck her how permanent and immobile everything looked. There were no sounds now. Not even the wind. The house and the landscape were one.

THEY DROVE up to the house in silence. Pippa sat at the front of the camper van this time, with her father, while the other two sat in the back, on bench seats. Bob Ford went ahead in a rusty mini pickup. A black and white bearded collie sat in the rear looking hot and bothered by everything, its long red tongue lolling. It watched them follow.

Sprog lowered her head as they neared the steps of the house. The building had reared up like a giant as they had pulled into the front drive. Now, she found herself having to stare upwards to take in all of the view.

Pippa was first out of the camper van this time. She ran round to the rear to unlock the door—the side door had never worked. Her spirits were brighter now. Perhaps it was something to do with her father's mood? She had heard him grit and grind his teeth when they had stood before the pond. Simply showing them the place had somehow been a necessary ritual she felt he would have preferred to avoid. He appeared relieved that the introduction was over.

"I'll put the girls' cases in the big room shall I, Mr Farris?" called Bob Ford. His roll up cigarette hanging from his lip.

"That will be fine," said Farris. "They can sort themselves out later, they're big enough." He nodded at Pippa, "least ways one of them is. Pippa's the chief 'imp'."

Pippa slapped her father on the arm.

The collie had already jumped from the rear of the pickup and was scurrying around the side of the building, barking at something in the bushes.

"Leave!" Bob Ford shouted, "Sally? Here bitch!"

The dog didn't return at first. Instead, it backed away from a thick tangle of privet, growling. It held its tail low.

Sprog watched the dog in silence, a finger raised to her lip as though telling the dog to be quiet.

"It'll be rabbits or summat," said Bob Ford, with a curt nod. "Sal—here—good bitch."

The dog turned away and made for the back of the mini pickup, where it quickly settled into a crouched position.

Bob Ford stroked his jaw.

Pippa busied herself, helping her father unload from the back of the camper van. There were several boxes of Sprog's toys. More than she would ever need, Pippa thought. She had even brought her much loved collection of soft animals. Frogs were the dominant creature, with three made of felt. Bella had just brought her clothes and her books, piled into a small tea chest.

Pippa fingered the spine of a book about stained glass, which stuck out from the corner of the chest. She gave a small murmur of satisfaction at seeing it and pulled the book up into a more prominent position. There was also a box of Sprog's colouring books, bought to encourage her to remain in one place due to her love of wandering. They never worked.

Farris went into the house. Instinctively, he headed for the kitchen and filled the kettle. He had drunk a lot of tea and coffee since his arrival.

Back outside, Sprog was looking over the place where the dog had been scratching and sniffing. She wondered if she might see the rabbit that it had found. She had noticed a pair of small red shining eyes within the hedge, but they had vanished after a moment or two with a shudder of leaves. Now there was only stillness.

With a disappointed sniff, she turned to see what the others were doing. Bella was struggling with a large piece of leather hand luggage.

Pippa called at her, from the doorway.

"Stephanie Farris: you could help, you know!"

Sprog hated her real name and made a growling noise in response, her tiny hands suddenly becoming claws.

"Come on sweetheart," called her father, who appeared behind her, "Pippa's right, don't leave it all up to her."

Bob Ford paused beside his mini to pat the dog and re-light his roll up cigarette. Farris went over to him.

"Daresay your girls go' more stuff than we moved into your workshop."

Farris chuckled.

"None of them will need it. They make their own amusement, they've always had to—at least for the past few years. Pippa helps me sometimes—is good at the work too. For most of the time she keeps watch on

Sprog—that's Stephanie. We call her Sprog, though. Mad about anything to do with frogs or anything that lives in a pond. Frog . . . Sprog . . . because she's so small, do you understand how . . . ?"

Bob Ford looked blank.

Farris resumed after a polite cough. "Bella alternates between reading and admiring her older sister."

"An' little un', the pond fiend, what does she do then?" Bob Ford made a gesture towards Sprog.

Farris shook his head.

"Sprog's just a pain in the arse," said Pippa, overhearing their conversation.

Farris was about to say something in reprimand, but stopped himself. Bob Ford was almost smiling, and that was a feat. He had been distant ever since Farris arrived. He was courteous, but Farris was certain that he didn't care for him being here. There had been times when Farris had wondered what he was doing here himself.

Sprog stood still for a moment, she felt dwarfed by all that was happening around her and wasn't sure that she liked being talked about in that way. Pippa's 'pain in the arse' was all right, but Bob Ford's 'little un' rang in her ears.

"I'm almost eight," she said indignantly, looking up at Bob Ford.

"Are you now? Thought you's was at least ten," he said with diplomacy. He raised an eyebrow while puffing silently at his cigarette.

Sprog smiled.

"Come on," said Pippa, pushing her father off the top step, and glaring at Sprog. "It's getting late and we've not even seen inside properly yet, you've just been messing about out here."

Sprog's smile spread wider, then she turned her head

upwards. The gables stared back down, the windows becoming eyes. For a moment, she lost her smile. A huge black bird, a jackdaw with its wings fluttering like a cape, was watching her from the roof.

TWO

BELLA INSISTED that they should all sleep together in the big room, across from what remained of the old library. It was the first room that she had discovered on her own, and took to it immediately, perhaps for that reason, but more likely because it looked grand and important.

The 'big room' was not ordinarily a bedroom, it had once served as a rear lounge. There was an impressive Adam fireplace, but little else of note other than its imposing size.

Once she had nosed around, Sprog decided that she preferred the more mysterious interior of the house, to the outside. She spent the first half an hour exploring some of the other downstairs rooms. A sweeping staircase started in the short hall, opposite the entrance. It led upstairs to a galleried landing and the main bedrooms. She had resisted the temptation to look upstairs, there was enough of interest on the ground floor. It was a huge adventure, a rabbit warren of passageways and closed doors. Glances round corners, and quick peeks into rooms, promised an interesting summer.

Bella spent several minutes simply standing in the centre of the big room, letting the sense of place creep in through her pores. She had watched her older sister do this many times, in old buildings. Pippa had always said that she was able to sense the 'spirit of the place'. The musty smell of the house lingered, it hung on the warm night air like distilled incense. There was a contagious oldness present, it wasn't just the dust, it was a quality that lived in the stone walls and timber floor boards almost within the soul of the house itself.

Bob Ford had been quick to get away, 'things to see to', he had explained. In the meanwhile, Pippa had helped her father move the big spare mattress into the chosen room.

Sprog kept running in front of the large French windows that looked out on to the garden. It was getting late now, and Pippa thought that the attraction of the game for her sister, was the sight of her reflection in the darkened glass. Something short had peered into the room, more than once. She wished that Sprog would stop the game, it was beginning to irritate her. Eventually, she shouted, and a reprimanded Sprog danced away, out into the kitchen.

They had a simple cold supper of ham and bread rolls in the kitchen. Afterwards, with a clap of his hands, Farris announced 'bedtime', and put Sprog on his shoulders to take her to the new bedroom.

He carried her out into the dark passageway, along to the room where Pippa had arranged their things. The others followed as though part of a procession. He bent down and clicked on the switch of a bedside table lamp, which balanced on the top of several of Bella's encyclopedias, beside the mattress.

When he put her down, Sprog pushed her fingers into her tee shirt and stretched it out in front of her, while twisting herself sideways. Pippa and Bella knew what was coming.

"Here comes the dance—the stamping of feet, the ritual," Pippa warned.

"Do I have to?" she whined, tilting her head a little to one side.

Bella was putting some of her things away into an interesting looking trunk that she had found. Now she was busy deciding which pajamas to wear.

Pippa marched over to Sprog, removed her fingers from the now knotted tee shirt bottom, and picked the little girl up into her arms. She gave her a big wet-sounding kiss on the forehead.

Sprog laughed, but objected all the same with a huge "Ugh!" Wishing to retain some sense of dignity, she wiped her forehead with her arm.

"Bed, mind the bugs don't bite."

Bella swept round with a sudden bounce and picked up her pajamas.

"Come on Stephanie Sproglodyte. I'll turn in early with you. Perhaps I might even read something to you, but only for a little while, I'm exhausted."

Sprog gave a saucy smile. The imp face came easily.

"And I'm knackered," she said.

"Stephanie!" cried Farris.

All three of the 'Imps' were as one. Farris stood back and watched them for a moment, and then joined in. He could hardly believe that they were his. His throat felt lumpy and when Pippa put Sprog down and wrapped her arms around him, once again he found it difficult.

LATER THAT evening Pippa and her father sat together in the kitchen. His overalls hung across a makeshift line, before a black and grimy cast iron boiler. A ray of beige light yawned across the room from the cracked shade of an old standard lamp. The remainder of their light came from a line of stumpy candles, fixed on chipped saucers. Farris had set these on the wooden work surface, beside the kitchen sink.

Shadows were everywhere: shapes that crossed and met like crazy paving. Folds of old brown wallpaper hung from the ceiling. Stacks of boxes and bottles threw their outline into this mixture too. Kit Farris' head was back-lit from the candle light, its shadow was larger than the rest and dominated the kitchen in a strangely reassuring way.

They hadn't seen each other since the beginning of term, before Farris went to Venice. When he had collected the three of them from the school it had been a special reunion for them all.

Now, at last, he felt settled, and Pippa was enjoying a moment of relief too. The murmurs that had escaped from the big room earlier, had finally drifted away like passing clouds, into sleep.

Neither had spoken, for what seemed like a very long time. Farris stroked his beard as if it were a furry pet. He stretched his legs, resting them on the edge of the table, toes poking through large holes, shamelessly.

Pippa cleared her throat and broke the silence.

He turned his head, with a quizzical expression across his face.

"Frog in the throat?"

Pippa cast her eyes upward.

"No, and please, not frogs."

"Oh yes—of course," he wiggled a big toe. "It was something to say."

"You look very tired," she replied. "Have you been sleeping okay?"

He looked towards the ceiling and rubbed his stiff neck with a growl. She noticed everything sometimes.

"Do I look that bad?"

She made a sound that suggested an uncommitted response.

"Well," he went on, "since you ask, no. I haven't been sleeping that well at all, I've been used to the cry of gondoliers as they passed by my window, not night owls and bats. But you girls should like it here, it may not be a luxury hotel but you've got to admit that the place does have a certain something."

"Sprog will run wild," Pippa said with a loose grin.

"Ah . . . Sprog," sighed her father. "Is she all right at school, was she okay after leaving your aunt? I suppose she's still scatty—Sprog I mean, not your aunt?"

"Sprog's fine—we all are, really. Sprog wanted to be with us. It's a good school, even if it is a bit stuffy. They even let Sprog indulge her frog habit. She has her collection on a kind of nature table in the corner of the classroom."

He gave an enigmatic smile and then went quiet, his face looked blank, unsure exactly what to say next. It was usually like this, his feeling lost for words. Normally it was just for the first few hours or so of a reunion. The guilty feeling was bubbling up again. He had always felt bad about taking off.

"You know I'd have you all with me if I could, you do know that, don't you? I mean regularly? There's good money abroad, you see, and I can get enough for us to . . ."

Pippa knew it was going to come up again eventually, but she'd rather it was mentioned on the first night. Then it was all said and out of the way. She hated watching him become tense and awkward, struggling to apologize yet again.

She crossed over to where he sat and crouched down beside his chair. She pulled at the sock with the largest hole.

"Of course we know. We really do like the school and Aunt Emma's as nice as anyone could be when we stay with her. We do get to see you a lot. There are some kids at the school who wouldn't recognize their parents if they bumped into them in the street—and that's when there's two of them. Alice, she's a new girl, last saw her father over a year ago. Mind you, I think there's something going on there." She tapped the side of her nose, knowingly. "This summer will be great, and you promised I could help you. I've been looking forward to that."

He suddenly looked better, the glow returning to his face like slowly warming coals.

"Of course." The serious look flashed into his face again. "The Venice job was important you know—good money. It was to make sure that you all wouldn't have to want for anything. It is a good school, too. Probably the best place for you all. And your aunt's good to you . . ."

His voice trailed off. Who was he trying to convince? There had been other reasons why he had to get away. Pippa patted her mouth and yawned.

"Boring," she groaned.

She shifted to another topic. "Tell me about this project, since I'm going to be a key member of the team."

Farris was about to reply when he suddenly raised his hand, and tilted his head to the side, listening for something.

"What . . .? What is it?" She asked.

He waved his fingers, gesturing to her to be quiet.

After a moment, he spoke up.

"Nothing, I thought I heard Sprog's voice, that was all."

Pippa frowned. Then she heard it too, a soft crying, but muffled, as though into a pillow.

"Sprog's just having a dream," Pippa decided. "It's if she starts to snore that we're all in trouble."

Her father's face had worried into a map of heavy lines. He didn't look as though he agreed with the explanation. A murmur, like a sudden low breeze, echoed somewhere behind the boiler. The sound ascended—as though sucked by a draft, up through the chimney. Outside the kitchen, the crying became a whimper and faded away.

The kitchen felt cold.

Father and daughter looked at one another and Pippa shrugged her shoulders.

"The wind," she continued, "hist whist as they say, hist whist . . . you were saying, or rather you weren't. The village? What's it like?"

Farris swallowed like a landed fish.

He got up from his chair and crossed to the stove. The hot plate was still piping. He moved the kettle on to it, after checking the weight to ensure it was filled.

"What about the village?" She asked again.

"Honingford's a friendly enough place, but I don't get to see anybody unless I go for things. I went into the village pub once, The Fox, it's by a cross roads. Seemed a good boozer but I didn't stay long. Friendly landlord though, keep's a good pint, well above average food and dogs everywhere. I was stared at a lot so I didn't go again."

He paused and looked up. It was obvious that his attention was still elsewhere.

"Go on," she urged.

He coughed hard and made an effort to concentrate.

"To be honest I'm left alone and that's the way I like it. Most of my visitors have been from the diocese office. The archdeacon popped his nose in once, when I first arrived. He introduced me to the assistant secretary, he's the man with my pocket money. Funny sort of bloke really, young and fussy with the most outrageous short back and sides haircut you've ever seen."

He stopped again. Pippa nodded.

"Name of Perkins, would you believe?"

She gave a snort.

"Where do the parishioners go while you're working?"

Farris looked puzzled.

"I mean for services," Pippa explained. "Is there another church?"

"Honingford folk don't use this church," he replied curtly. "Didn't I say? They haven't in over a 100 years."

"Why?"

Farris looked blank.

"I don't really know. Decline in the numbers of church-goers, didn't like the sermons they were getting. It's not unusual, and you know how many churches there are in East Anglia. A lot. Church people go to another village."

He paused for a moment yet again.

"Then why are you doing this work?" Pippa asked. "I mean surely if the church isn't . . . ."

"Restoration. Historical interest of course!" He interrupted with a sudden nervousness.

"Sorry?"

He got up and went over to the sink. Selecting two of the cleanest looking mugs from the drainer, he ran hot water and rinsed them.

"Historical interest," he repeated, over his shoulder. "That's why I'm here. The job has come out of the redundant churches fund. The church is of architectural and historical importance. The job should have been carried out years ago, but was repeatedly put off. The new diocese man wants his books straight and up to date and the money is still sitting there, they have to spend it. So . . . The glass is interesting at any rate—what's left of it."

He turned off the tap and stared ahead.

"Very interesting indeed."

There was a brief period of silence again. Several stumpy candles had snuffed out, the kitchen had become the colour of brown wash. Pippa watched the wispy trails of smoke weave upwards.

"Who was that man we saw?" she asked, changing the subject.

"Who?" Her father poured the hot water into a fresh

pot of tea.

"That man with the dog, the one who was supposed to help us move in but just smoked a badly made cigarette. Bob Ford—wasn't that his name?"

"Oh, he's all right. Bob kind of acts as a caretaker for several churches, does gardening more than anything else to be honest. His family has lived in the village for donkey's years. He just wanted to give you the once over, that's all. Stands and stares a lot. You'll soon get used to it.

"It sounds as if you've had a lonely time here."

"Not really," he smiled, handing her a mug. "I've made a friend or two."

His eyes twinkled, he was relaxing.

She put her mug down and stretched her arms around his shoulders. She pushed her face into his chest. Pippa could smell the leather apron from his jumper, the hint of pipe tobacco. She hugged him hard, her ear squeezing against him. His heart thudded like an engine.

"I have missed you. We all have."

Her fingers dug into his back.

"And I've missed you too, sweetheart," he whispered in return.

The wind whistled somewhere behind them.

From outside the kitchen, there came the sound of crying, again. Softer this time, away in the distance. She felt him twitch, as if a nerve in his neck had been pinched.

Pippa pulled back.

"It's only Sprog again, I'll just check."

"I'm sure it's nothing," he insisted. "It'll be all right . . . don't . . ."

But she was halfway through the door, before Farris could finish.

"Hurry back . . . hurry or . . . or your tea will get cold."

The passageway was heavy with gloom. A hazy white

line crept out from beneath the door of the big room. There were only the sounds of silence.

Pippa tiptoed over to the door and turned the large round china knob. She peeked in. All was still.

The cry came again, but this time it was behind her, and it came from a place at the top of the stairs.

She turned and looked upwards.

The cry stirred echoes.

She felt herself suddenly pulled back to a time, earlier in the day. One of Sprog's toy animals had fallen from a packing case, its head jammed in the camper van door when they slammed it shut. Sprog and the others had just laughed, but Pippa had not.

The cry faded.

A shudder passed through her. She wondered whether she should go and see what it was, but the landing was poorly lit, and anyhow, how could it be anyone? The family was, after all, downstairs.

"Hist whist," she whispered. "Just nothing, nothing at all."

She turned and hurried back.

Her father was unsmiling. They caught a certain look in one another's eyes.

"What was it?" he asked. There was an ill-hidden note of anxiety in his voice.

"Nothing, maybe it was nothing at all," she replied, wondering if he knew more. Then she added, "it wasn't Sprog though."

Farris, already pale, turned a shade whiter.

THREE

BELLA ENTERED the kitchen to find that her father had been up and about for some time. The coffee pot was almost empty and the breakfast table was strewn with multiple butter knives, soiled with the remains of jam or marmalade spread, and in one case, with both.

Reading spectacles were perched at the end of Farris' nose, and he was staring hard at a butter greased sketch. The large sheet lay untidily on top of a half-eaten piece of toast. He appeared to have dressed in a hurry, wearing a disheveled-looking white polo sweater and jeans, and with his hair unbrushed. Bella however, was still in her pajamas.

There was an early morning chill in the air that made the quarry-tiled floor colder. For a moment Bella hopped from one foot to the other, hoping that this would warm up the soles of her bare feet.

Farris stared at her over his spectacles, looking, for one moment, as if he didn't know who she was.

"Bel? Give me a kiss," he grunted.

She pulled her long brown hair back over her shoulders, pushed her round face into Farris', and blew a raspberry kiss into his beard.

"Why are you up so early?" he asked, "I thought you'd all be sleeping in."

"Too much to do," she chirped, helping herself to the remains of her father's piece of toast.

"Oh yes, like what?"

"Oh, like exploring the Grange, making sure that Sprog doesn't get into any trouble. You know, molesting rare examples of pond life, crested newt and the like. Keeping her out of that pond water for a start I suppose. Do you know how deep it is? It's more like a pool than a pond."

He put his sketch to one side.

"Nope, and by the way, I meant to speak to you about Sprog."

He patted the chair beside him and poured her a glass of orange juice. Just as he replaced the jug he looked up, startled. From somewhere else in the house came the sound of running feet and Pippa's voice, calling out to Sprog. Farris didn't catch what she said, but it was a sisterly warning. It was something to do with toothpaste and one's behaviour with it, judging from the tone of her voice.

"Before they find us," continued Farris, lowering his voice, almost to a whisper. "I promised Pippa that she could help me with some restoration work at St Mary's."

Bella lowered her head and moved forward, nodding slowly.

"And," he continued, "it means that for much of the time she'll either be in the workshop here with me, or in the church."

"That's fine, I've got things I can . . ."

"Well," he interrupted. "It's just that . . . Well now that you're getting older—a teenager next September remember, I thought you might take some weight off Pippa regarding our Sprog. Keep even more of an eye on her, you know what I mean, don't you? This is a working holiday I'm afraid, and this is an old house—rambling and some rooms are almost in a state of collapse. Then there's the garden . . ."

Bella murmured in agreement, sounding like a crusty magistrate who had just grasped an important fact in a case.

She lowered her voice.

"I've already started to look after Sprog, you know."

He caught his breath. Of course she had, he realized.

"Don't worry, Daddy," she continued, "I know she's a handful."

Farris resisted a laugh.

Then Bella turned her face fully towards her father's.

"Pippa's already spoken to me about all that anyway, before we came here. We had a special discussion."

"Oh, I see."

Farris felt peculiarly redundant for a moment. He patted his daughter on the back of her head and turned away. Bella trotted over to the kitchen door and with a 'see you later' call, left without touching her orange juice.

He was alone.

A voice from his thoughts darted in, a sudden unwelcome fear.

'They don't need me.'

He shook his head as if to remove the idea.

Suddenly, he remembered his wife, their mother, Isabel. He saw her lying on the downstairs' couch. Pippa was then the same age as Bella was now. She was always busy, bringing and fetching things for her mother, caring and loving. Perhaps doing his job for him, even then. It was Pippa who would quietly close the sitting room door, if Bella came charging into the house with friends. "Isabel," he said softly.

This was the hardest thing about being with the children; the ease with which they prompted memories, mostly without warning. For several seconds his wife's face: sallow cheeks and high forehead, the same as his eldest daughter's, floated into view before him. He closed his eyes. The face remained.

"Pippa," he said.

"Dad?" Came the reply from the doorway.

*   *   *

FARRIS HAD breakfast again. He didn't mind. The second time he shared the excitement and laughter of his 'three imps'. Wishing to get started, he issued house rules on morning routine. Bella took her role seriously, and managed to maneuver Sprog into standing still.

"The rules are basic," he began. "One, keep to the grounds. Two, go only into those rooms in this part of the house. Three, if you go into the church, which I'll show you later, remember it is not a playground. Right?"

Sprog and Bella agreed.

Pippa added a few afterthoughts, to 'the permitted Sprog and Bella territory' guidelines. She even managed to phrase the ideas so that Farris thought that they might have been his. At 8 a.m. Farris announced that they should get dressed, and prepare for the day.

Sprog kept wandering up the staircase, unable to resist the lure of secret rooms, while her sisters spent ages in the bathroom. Farris washed up at the kitchen sink, where he kept soap and a toothbrush amongst soap pads and dish cloths. From here he could keep one ear open, just in case.

After Bella had helped Sprog finally decide which pair of shorts she wanted to wear, they reassembled in the kitchen.

"A quick tour then?" suggested Farris, "just so that we all know what's what."

Sprog's face lit up and for a moment he wondered if a further tooth might have gone missing.

He led the way into a rear hall, behind the kitchen.

"This was the games room once," he announced, pushing open a paint-blistered door.

"Games!" exclaimed Sprog, the mere mention of the word was enough to secure her ever-wandering attention.

"In olden days," said Bella authoritatively, "in big houses, they could sometimes afford to set a whole room aside."

"Quite right," said Farris, "but games room has turned into work room for now, okay?"

He pushed the door wide and Sprog's smile grew at the hugeness of the place, bigger even than their bedroom. In the centre was a large work table for cutting, covered with the usual thick green felt that their father used to support the glass. To the right was a smaller table, littered with various pots of enamel, brushes and other bottles. Behind this, was fixed some makeshift shelving, where sections of lead strip lay with coils of solder.

Pippa marched up to the table and looked beneath the top.

"What . . . what is it?"

"I was lucky," snorted Farris, "it's an old billiard table, I found it dumped out the back in a cutting shed. I put a board on the top, unrolled my felt, and was away."

"What about a kiln?" she asked, glancing quickly about her.

"I could hardly bring that with me, could I? Well I've made a special contact. The architect arranged it. There's a potter near here, a Miss Prestwood—Sarah's her name. I've got an arrangement, she lets me fire at her studio."

"Sarah?" mocked Pippa, "an arrangement, eh?"

"She's . . . well she's very nice," Farris said, inadequately. "You'll meet her."

"Dad's got a lady friend!" said Sprog, immediately picking up on this snippet and then dancing across the room to the garden window.

Farris suddenly felt embarrassed and cast his head downward.

Bella found sheets of coloured glass, stacked on felt

pads, beside the window. Farris noticed her fingering the edge of a sheet of deep royal blue.

"Careful," he called. "You don't want a band aid on your very first day, do you?"

Pippa had finished looking over the contents of an open drawer, and was now staring at a rectangular shaped object, covered with a clean, but paint-stained cloth. It stood on an easel construction, and measured about four foot by three; she thought it might be a frame clamp. As she reached out towards it, she hesitated, as if the cover might conceal a secret portrait, unready for another's eyes.

She turned towards her father, expecting an automatic explanation.

"It's a window I've been working on," he volunteered. "Very detailed work. There's a fair bit of restoration to do all round in this church. I have to make a new window— possibly two. Victorian glass, the lot of it. The central section that this replaces is badly damaged."

Pippa went to remove the cover.

"Not yet," he cautioned. Her hand froze mid-way. "Let me show you the church first."

"I do want to see it though," she insisted. "You know how interested I always am in what you're doing."

He felt a sudden pride.

"There's traditional here, but with other styles, images you might not expect in a church."

He beamed enthusiastically for the first time, just like he used to.

"What's particularly unique though," he went on, "is that the work was carried out by the parish priest himself, then later by an agent of his."

Pippa was hooked. Her father usually had good stories to tell, they came with the work.

"You mean he made his own windows?"

"Well, not all of them. I got some of his story from the diocese secretary. I tried to find out more from the people in the village, but nobody was interested in helping. He did a fair bit of the work in the early days, but apparently as he got older he developed a problem with his hands. He couldn't hold things properly, or something like that. So he used his own craftsman, brought him in from somewhere—he wasn't a local man, in fact I can't find out where the chap came from, but he was good. Damn good. Some of his stuff was very unusual, reminiscent of a medieval style, funnily enough. The story goes, that this man remained here, right up to the time the clergyman moved on."

Farris stroked his beard, in deep thought.

"They liked to place little narrative pieces around the edges of the larger windows. They're a bit odd, the scenes that is."

Sprog became bored and skipped to the other side of the room. Bella, like her older sister, was captivated.

"What do you mean, odd?" asked Bella.

"Never mind," he sighed.

"Go on," demanded Pippa.

"Some panes are broken, I suspect vandalised, it's difficult to follow the story line in many of them at times, if there really is one. A huge section of the middle of this window has gone. I would say it was a piece composed by both of our clergyman and his assistant. The thing's given me a headache, style matching and so on." He pause and looked up. "Sorry, like I said, I'll show it to you later."

Pippa turned away, she would have to be patient. She walked over to join Sprog, who was staring intently out of the window, something had caught her attention in the garden.

"Who was this clergyman?" asked Bella.

"Didn't I tell you?" He felt in his pocket for his pipe. "The Reverend Dr Chauncey Barrow."

"Chauncey?" repeated Bella, wrinkling her nose at the sound of the name.

A sudden cry from Sprog interrupted them.

"Daddy, what's that?"

Farris and Bella wheeled round together. They joined the other two at the window. Sprog was pointing across to the rear stretch of lawn. Like the front of the house, high privet hedges bordered the garden, overtaken on the right hand stretch by a great twist of bindweed.

Farris wasn't certain what it was that his daughter was pointing to.

"What?" he asked.

"I don't know what you're pointing at, either!" said Pippa impatiently.

"Where that man waved," persisted Sprog, also faintly irritated.

"Man?" Farris asked, deciding it must be the gardener. "Bob's early, and I wasn't even sure that he was coming over today."

He looked past his daughters, but could see nobody.

"That grey thing up in the corner," Sprog continued.

Farris craned his neck and finally realized what she meant. In the far corner of the lawn within another, shorter run of hedge, was a cylindrical shape.

"You've got good eyesight young lady," Farris sniffed. "Do you mean that pillar thing? What made you ask about that?"

"I told you Daddy. The man waved."

Sprog mumbled something beneath her breath. Having lost interest by causing such an unexpected fuss, she twirled around and ran over to the covered easel.

"Don't touch that!" hissed Bella.

Sprog pulled a face and continued out of the room, in search of other adventures.

Farris remained staring through the window. He did not know what the grey pillar was. He scanned the rest of the garden. A large weeping willow to the left, swayed with the morning breeze, its branches almost kissed the grass. A central oval of simple flowers, marigolds and bedding plants broke the plain. Two stone pedestals stood on either side, a be-headed statue was fixed to the top on one, and a bowl on the other. It might have been a bird bath. Shadows slid across the lawn, cast there from the hedge. The day promised fine weather, but a strangeness had settled across the scene. Now he wanted to discover if there was anyone out there who shouldn't be. He clenched his fist and turned away.

FOUR

KIT FARRIS conducted a short tour of the rest of the Grange. He led them around the neatly kept garden, which fronted the pond, moving casually but swiftly, with his hands behind his back. He talked at them, rather than with them, as they walked, his attention clearly elsewhere.

Farris explained that before Dr Barrow's time, the place had been the rectory for a clergyman who had a large family. The house was once divided into several self-contained sections. Servants or housekeepers lived in one part of the house, and the other rooms were for the family and guests. A Sunday school had been held in a large upstairs room, or so the diocese secretary thought. Dr Barrow had continued running the classes for a little while after he took over, but eventually his numbers fell and the school was abandoned. Dr Barrow remained living there, alone with his assistant.

They now moved to the rear garden, which the workshop overlooked.

"The Grange suited me though," concluded Farris as they walked out to the centre of the lawn. "It's right next to the job, I could set up a place to work and we'd be left alone, and I thought you'd think it a fun place for the summer."

Pippa linked his arm.

"And it won't matter so much if Sprog destroys everything. It's great."

The other two hurried ahead of them. He had been anxious to get outside to nose around, without wishing to alarm the girls. His tour had enabled him to do that, and now he had peace of mind.

Bella and Sprog were taken with the willow tree, Sprog kept jumping up at the branches, trying desperately to find one low enough to swing from. Teasing her, Bella had managed to reach a strong limb without too much trouble.

Farris and Pippa walked towards the far corner. He wanted to discover the cylindrical thing for himself.

Pippa saw it before Farris was even certain that they were heading in the right direction. She unlinked her arm and ran ahead. When he joined her, she was already pushing and pulling away the branches of the hedge. It had grown particularly thickly here and there was an uncharacteristic lack of maintenance in this patch.

"Bob Ford's forgotten this bit by the look of it," said Pippa, stamping down the more stubborn branches.

Within a few minutes, the grey, moss-covered stone, became an ornate pillar. Fine web-like fissures wove a glistening pattern of cracks across the surface. It had a flat pedestal top to it, with a central circular area, now a mossy slime green. The base disappeared into the undergrowth, but widened into a stone platform.

"What is it?" she asked.

Farris did not reply. Instead, dropping his glasses down on to the end of his nose, he examined the top, scraping away some moss with his finger nail.

"This is stubborn stuff to move," he murmured. "I think I know what I'm going to find, though."

The moss didn't seem to want to come away. He scratched harder, and then suddenly sighed between tightly clenched teeth.

"What is it?" Pippa asked.

He lifted his finger to his mouth and sucked.

"Must have caught it on something," he mumbled.

He took his finger from his mouth and examined the

nail. A tiny dewdrop of red squeezed slowly out from the tip, mixing with a stain of green.

She pulled his finger towards her and sneered.

"Wimp. You'll live."

"It's almost certainly a sundial," Farris declared, brushing his hands together. The dial's missing though, that's what I was after. Pity. Must say it's the largest I've ever seen. Strange. I mean, what is it doing hidden away here?"

"Perhaps this hedge hasn't always been here?" suggested Pippa. "Overgrown with time, something like that?"

Farris wasn't sure. He was about to examine it further, when he cocked his head to one side as though he had heard something. Quickly, he moved past Pippa, scrambling through the hedge to where the grass was less well kept. He scanned across from the hedgerow to the pathway that led to the house.

There was no sign of anybody. Even the breeze had died away, and the pond water was its usual eerie stillness.

He turned his gaze to the clump of trees that hid the view of the church. Suddenly he remembered something and glanced at his watch.

"I've got a meeting," he announced, feeling very disorganized. "I must go."

As he turned, a cry came unexpectedly from the other side of the hedge.

"Sprog!" It was Bella's voice and it sounded urgent.

Pippa reacted immediately and fought her way through the tangle of green.

Farris's heart suddenly rose in his chest.

Pushing his face into the hedgerow, after Pippa, he clawed the branches aside and hurried back to the garden. He was in time to see Pippa running towards the willow tree, where Bella was jumping up and down excitedly at the bottom.

"What . . . what is it, what's happened?" he called as he ran across the lawn.

When he arrived at the tree, he felt a surge of emotions, relief initially—but tempered because his youngest daughter was perched in a very precarious place.

He looked upwards, into the tree's umbrella cover.

There, at the highest point, arms waving amongst the branches, was Sprog.

"Come down!" yelled Bella, as Pippa jumped for the nearest branch.

"Daddy, Daddy!" called Sprog excitedly. "No hands, see?"

FIVE

FARRIS HUGGED Sprog, pulling her roughly into his arms, loving and scolding her at one and the same time. She could have fallen from the tree so easily. For a moment he wondered if having them with him was such a good idea after all. Sprog's large eyes told him that it was.

He instructed Bella, charging her with the task of keeping her little sister under firmer control. The garden was to be the sole extent of their territory until he said otherwise, and tree climbing was strictly not allowed. Pippa quietly told Bella of the find at the corner of the garden. She hoped that the sundial might serve to occupy Sprog, if she became bored.

They walked back to the house.

"I only wanted to see Daddy's church from the top of the tree," Sprog moaned, after Bella had brushed leaves from her hair.

"In time, very soon in fact," said Farris, putting his pipe nervously into his mouth for the first time that morning. He suddenly realized he had seldom lit it.

He stopped as they reached the back door and lit his pipe. His eyelids drooped peacefully after the first few puffs of tobacco smoke. The pipe complemented the sense of relief that he was feeling. He knew he should give up, especially with the kids now being here. For a moment, Pippa thought that he was going to remain standing there all morning.

She pulled her father to his senses with a gentle tug of the arm.

"Only old men smoke pipes," she said.

Ignoring her comment he picked up his bag of tools

and papers that he had left outside the door. Pippa turned to the others.

"Dad's got a meeting," she declared. "I'll be back shortly. Stay out of trouble."

Bella firmly held Sprog's shoulders so that she was positioned directly in front of her father.

"Remember Pippa's words," Farris warned Sprog, and indicated to Pippa that they should go.

They hurried across the lawn in the direction of the church. His mind was racing with a thousand and one thoughts: child minding, restoration, strange sundials, church officials.

"Cut through the clump, there," he mumbled, as they crossed a patchy stretch of sun scorched grass and wild flowers. It took them no time at all.

Through the trees, beyond the greens and browns of leafy clusters, which formed a natural sanctuary, Pippa saw a mosaic of coloured stone. The flint rubble construction was a multiple of shades: blues and browns with beiges and yellows, all different textures. The flint sparkled with spots of crystal, like gem stones, caught in glimpses of bright sunshine.

The church had a square tower, cornered by stocky angle buttresses, punctuated by a series of small rectangular windows. Trees veiled the top of the tower. The place looked mysterious, partnering the Grange perfectly.

"Very early site," Farris volunteered, stopping for a moment. He bit at his pipe stem. "Roman, in fact. There's a churchyard at the back, it was once supposed to be bounded by part of the outer moat of a castle. I can't find any castle round here now, though. The Abbey must have been near here, nothing at all left of that, either. The whole site makes up what was known as the Monk's 'quarter'. This land was given over specially, by the Monastery."

"Steeped in history then?" she said. "I like that."

"The south doorway is probably Norman," he declared, getting into his stride. "Adapted in the 14th century and given a pointed arch. Additions over the next few hundred years I'd have said, but the place underwent a major restoration in the second half of the 19th century. That was when they put the stained glass in, of course."

"What are we going to do today?" Pippa had adopted an efficient tone of voice.

"Well," he began. "I don't really want to leave Sprog and Bella alone for too long. I have got work to do on that window, too. The meeting is with the architect who's keeping one eye on the job for the diocese committee. You might get to see Mr Perkins, if you're lucky."

"So it's all chat and back?"

"Not quite," he said. "There's a bit of cementing to be done and I've got to take out a lower panel from up on a scaffolding board. Come on."

Pippa screwed up her face as they continued through the trees.

"Cementing!"

"You want to learn don't you? Well that's important, we can't have the glass rattling about like a set of false teeth."

"I don't mind really," she replied. "It's just such a filthy job."

"Why d'you think you've got it?"

He winked and strode ahead of her, clambering playfully over the short picket fence that preceded the boundary, and into the grounds of St Mary's.

PIPPA AND Farris arrived at the front of the church to

discover that the diocese architect was already waiting. He had been met by the secretary, Mr Perkins. Farris introduced Pippa to both of them, and made apologies for being late. The architect assured him that it was they who had been early.

The church official and the architect were as different as chalk and cheese. Pippa thought that the architect looked exactly as she expected. He was introduced as David Mellor, and wore a dark suit with a blue tie, snugly pulled against a hard white collar. An obviously new leather attaché case was tucked beneath his arm. His face was a beam of bright eye, combined with a wide crocodile smile of teeth. She thought he was attractive, but was not so sure that he was someone she would trust.

The diocese secretary suddenly shuffled forwards. Pippa thought Mr Perkins was a real find. He was a young man, but he had a manner that made him seem old. A well-greased fringe fell before his eyes, like an untidy pelmet. His laugh sounded small and terribly nervous and his head bobbed from side to side, in peril of snapping from his neck. He was also dressed in a suit, but whereas Mellor was relaxed and at ease in his, Mr Perkins appeared hot and uncomfortable. A scruffy tie was pulled to one side, with an ill-tied knot. Despite there being no real warmth from the sun yet, he had broken out into a sweat.

After introductions they stared at one another blankly. Pippa struggled to hold back a laugh. Farris prayed that she would be able to control herself.

"Mmm, mmm, well, I always say: work to do, work to do." Mr Perkins tittered again and made a funny sound in his throat, like a small bird.

Pippa waited for him to lead the way, but he looked down at his legs as though unsure what movement they should make.

He flickered his eyelids at Pippa.

"After you, mmm, after you indeed. Ladies before gentlemen, eh? Mmm, mmm."

The irritating titter rattled out of him, again.

Farris caught the impatient roll of Mellor's eyes.

"Here," Farris said, eager to advance the proceedings. "The door's unlocked. I don't make a habit of locking up after me, unless there's something I particularly want to secure."

Mr Perkins pulled a face at hearing this. He looked surprised and slightly disapproving, but said nothing.

A twist of the massive iron ring handle creaked the heavy yew door inwards.

The echo of their footsteps was sharp and clear. Mr Perkins' metal capped shoes rang out on the brick floor. The musty smell of ancient stone and a trace of something else, like decayed incense, filled their nostrils. An uneasy silence fell about the place as they stood still. Pippa took in the atmosphere of antiquity with a series of long and lingering murmurings, as she looked about her. She loved 'oldness'.

The church was small, but of a more generous size than was usual for a rural village. In the south-west corner a dusty organ had been set into the wall. A handsome roof crowned the nave, with a series of tie-beams and collar beams and much traceried woodwork.

She walked slowly to the north arcade and allowed her fingers to trace a line along a stone pier. Holding her face closer to the surface she tried to see what was cut into the stone. There were faces, a box shape with somebody lying in it, very crudely drawn, and what appeared to be various signatures.

She heard the titter behind her. It startled her and she

turned with a gasp.

"Excuse me, oh, mmm, mmm, I didn't mean . . ." Mr Perkins looked embarrassed. "That is 12th and 16th century graffiti Miss Farris. We think so anyway."

He looked pleased with himself at the explanation. Then he added.

"It's everywhere you know. Children did it, I wouldn't doubt."

"They could write then, in those days, children I mean?" she frowned at him.

He wasn't sure what to say. He turned towards Farris who was standing at the bottom of the aisle with the architect.

Pippa looked back over the graffiti. There were some longer messages along one side of the pier. Someone had written a quotation: *'They lie in wait to deceive.'* Beneath this was added: *'May the Lord God save us'*.

She repeated the quotation softly to herself. The words almost tasted salty on her lips.

Mr Perkins called over to Farris.

"Your daughter, mmm," Perkins mused, smiling, "obviously captivated by all of this. Delightful to see, mmm, most delightful and so rare in the young these days. That's what I say. So very, very rare."

"She's a potential antiquarian," smiled Farris. He walked over to join them. "Get her into an antique shop and she'll be happy for hours, but get her into a building with really old and interesting stuff, and you've had it. I think she got most of it from her mother." He glanced down for a moment. "My wife was a historian—a conservationist."

Then he added quietly.

"She died three years ago."

Mr Perkins made an awkward gesture with a waving of

the hand, which Farris took to be some kind of indication of condolence.

"And, mmm," Mr Perkins continued, nodding nervously, "to follow in father's footsteps, eh, eh?"

"We'll see," said Farris.

Pippa glanced up at him.

"I have a little interest, mmm, in history myself. Local you know, wherever I happen to be working or staying. Mmm. I'm just about to go as far back as I can with this site. Finding out things I mean. I'm new to this diocese— got to get things in their place, as I always say. The restoration should have been completed years ago. Sloppy, sloppy, and the place is so interesting. Mmm, fascinating, fascinating."

"Even though nobody comes here?" Mellor interjected.

"A monument to history, sir," said Perkins, with some measure of indignation. "We must have everything tidy, and after all, the money for the project has sat without call. In fact I think we should have probably lost the allocation a long time ago. Better use it up before we're found out, eh?"

Pippa cocked her head to one side.

"There was an abbey near here, so Dad explained?"

"Oh indeed, indeed. Mmm. But the site is very ancient. Very. All sorts of interesting stories I believe. It's getting them to the surface that's the problem. Eh?"

He tittered and snorted at the same time.

"The monks had a special input to St Mary's, you know, mmm, especially when they carried out their additional building works. They used a few of their people.

"The archdeacon mentioned to me that they had a particularly gifted monk. He went by the name of Master Edric: made the most beautiful pictures, did Books of Hours, paintings, carvings and so on. Yes, mmm. He was charged to work here on some of his designs by the sub-sacrist. That was the monk in charge of the building works. Mmm. Something went wrong though. It was strange. It's what I find so interesting, a mystery you see. His designs were used in the church and in a collection of special manuscripts housed in the abbey library. He spent much time at St Mary's and was buried around here somewhere at first. But not long afterwards they discovered something about him, alleged misdeeds. Something that was scandalous, yes, mmm. Yes, indeed."

Mr Perkins' face lit up for a moment as though he secretly approved of scandal.

"This discovery was so awful that the abbot ordered that they burn his books, destroy all traces of his work in the church. He was taken out of his burial place and moved to unconsecrated ground. Mmm. It sounds awful. Delicious story though, delicious."

"What had he done?" asked Pippa.

Mr Perkins giggled.

"Mmm. That's the fun bit. I don't know. I'm jolly well going to find out, though!"

His face shone like a small schoolboy's as he only just managed to hold himself back from breaking out into a guffaw.

"Let us know when you do," said Farris.

Mellor took a discreet look at his watch and coughed.

"Mr Farris, there was something you wanted to query with us I understand?"

Mr Perkins looked distinctly put out for a moment, but re-adjusted the knot in his tie, flicked back his fringe with a toss of his head and walked briskly back along the aisle to join the architect.

"Yes, it won't take long," said Farris turning to the side aisle.

Pippa stopped tracing her fingers across the surface of the pier and continued to look around her. The church was in a reasonable condition considering it was no longer used. All traces of Master Edric's work had long been removed. One wall had been restored recently and the surface re-coated with a white wash. Above the aisles, rows of windows displayed a somber but rich array of colours. Blue and gold panels of glass set within complex webs of borders of lead strip.

She hadn't noticed the windows when first she entered the church, and yet, from the interior these were without a doubt the most striking feature of the place.

Looking towards the rear of the church, most of the panes to her left were thick with grime, or cracked with many sections either missing or badly broken. Opposite, the signs of her father's patient skills were clear. A row of windows sparkled with fresh colour, but they retained the sense of age which Pippa found so attractive.

The line of scaffolding boards obscured a complete view of the windows. She craned her neck and stood on tip-toe to try and obtain a better view. There were two smaller panes that may have been designed to emphasize the larger frame of concrete. The clear blue of the morning sky looked through the arched gap.

She looked back to where her father and the two officials stood huddled over some of his sketches.

"Can I go up?" she called, pointing towards the scaffold.

"Be careful, " said Farris.

Their heads re-huddled.

Pippa slid between the pews, down towards the right tower against which had been tied a rung ladder. With her view fixed upwards she slowly climbed to the top of the scaffold.

The boards were not fixed particularly high, but as she stepped onto the top walkway, the view below her began to swim. She stretched out her hand to reach for a scaffolding pole, but missed. Suddenly, she fell forward, only just managing to regain her balance. A dungarees buckle, scraped against the pole.

Farris looked upwards, with a start.

"Hey! Be careful!" She heard her father's voice from below.

The sunlight warmed her face as it streamed through the concrete frame. It brought her back round.

"I'm . . . I'm all right," she replied.

Her mouth felt dry, and she blinked hard for a few seconds to bring herself properly together.

"Just me being heavy footed."

The men below all stared together with faces like a trio of monkeys, then they returned to huddle round the drawing.

Pippa looked out from the space, across an overgrown churchyard to the tree boundary. Through a break in the trees she could see the village, with the pretty thatch-covered houses amidst the reds and blacks of pantiles. It was a peaceful setting, but she thought, remote from the church and its grounds, as though set apart by reasons other than distance. She noticed a few stones, gathered into mounds that cast animal-shaped shadows on to the grass. They might have been buildings once, now they looked like strange solitary monuments.

She suddenly fancied that the place was shunned.

She turned her attention to the windows. Her father had been working his way along the aisle, restoring each pane in its turn. The windows to the right were in a similar condition to those opposite. She doubted that the job would be completed by the end of the summer.

She recognized some scenes, they were the usual biblical references. The far window showed the risen Christ with the women and two apostles at the tomb. She thought it was likely to be Victorian, but altogether in a different style to the preceding windows, which were very badly broken. To her immediate right there appeared to be a gathering of Roman soldiers, who surrounded a crouched figure. Their spears pointed inwards, as if in defence. Part of the subject that occupied their attention was missing. The lower half, where the limbs of the figure curled inwards, ended in a mis-shapen strip of lead.

Above the window, in a separate frame was a quotation: *'Those that look out of the windows be darkened.'*

She read it again, without understanding what it meant.

For some while she stared at the remains of the crouched figure, wondering suddenly whether it was a person at all. She fancied it was an animal, but deformed and curled into itself.

She leaned across the end scaffolding pole and tried to touch the glass. It moved easily, but the surface felt slippery, as though covered in a layer of grease. She scraped a little with her nail and the dirty beige revealed another, brighter colour, beneath.

"Not been cleaned in some while," she mumbled to herself in disgust.

The daylight showed brighter, shining through a section of green, the size of a halfpenny piece.

With a resolute smack of her lips she looked over the other windows. For the first time she noticed that there were more quotations and sayings fixed in the upper frames. Many were unreadable, either through being so dirty, or having sections cracked or missing.

She could easily read the one above the missing

window, contained in a frame of iron:

"Light of moon be as light of sun."

An unusual nodule of green coloured glass, which looked like a large marble or a crystal, was set within a design that reminded her of an eye. This occupied a separate circular section of window at the peak of the stone arch. Above this, engraved into the stone was the line:

"Mine eye shall see my desire."

The etched lettering was clear and unclogged.

Again, she wondered what this could mean, and then she tried to imagine what kind of picture might have been below.

"What was in here?" she called over her shoulder.

For a moment no answer came and then she heard her father's footsteps. She looked down and saw that he was alone, she hadn't been aware that the others had left.

"Where are . . .?"

He raised his finger to his lips.

"Be polite, they're only outside. They're standing below the windows along from where you are. I asked if they could arrange for some halogen lamps to be fixed on the outer wall."

"Why do you want lamps?" She asked.

"I'm envisaging putting in some late hours, they'll be better than the torch if I've got to come and go. The grounds can be as black as soot if there's cloud."

She screwed her face into a mask of playful mockery.

"You're scared of the dark!"

Farris looked uncomfortable with the jibe. She caught the look on his face.

"Dad! You *are* afraid!" She was surprised but amused at the same time. Then she realized that the graveyard would become floodlit and somehow the funnier side of her taunting became lost.

"You asked me something?" he continued, changing the subject.

"Oh, yes," she jerked her head towards the window space. "What went in there?"

"Funny you should ask, that's the reason I've had this meeting this morning. I needed agreement to continue with the work on that."

"Why?"

He hesitated, sometimes he found her directness more than a little unsettling. "Because so much of the original has gone, and I'm not entirely certain what should replace it. A central figure is incomplete, but let me show you back at the house, that's where the frame is."

"Did they give you the okay?" She persisted.

He laughed.

"Yes, yes, they gave me the okay, and without even looking at the original."

She detected an air of cynicism in his voice.

"Dad?"

He put his finger to his lips again.

"I'll tell you later."

He motioned towards the open window and she realized that the men outside could probably hear every word they were saying. She made a Laurel and Hardy nod of 'mum's the word', and started to make her descent back down on to the ladder.

A few moments later, Farris heard his name called from outside the front door. He turned to re-join the diocese officials.

Pippa heard the nervous titter again and the more confident laughter of Mellor the architect. She decided not to re-join her father to wave goodbye. Instead she stood quietly, allowing herself to blend with the place for a moment. She wanted to try and get beneath the skin of it. There was something about this church that didn't seem right and it annoyed her that she couldn't decide what it was.

SIX

SPROG SAT outside in the garden. Her crayons lay beside her and the drawing pad, which was newly started, rested against hunched legs. She had been trying to draw the boundary of the garden, beyond the willow tree. The hedgerow was outlined in a dark green, and the same colour was used to shade in patches of shadow. Above this the horizon was drawn with a pale blue. She had intended to sketch in the weeping willow tree next.

Sprog frowned.

She lowered her knees a little to take another look at the view, and satisfied that there was nothing hiding in the hedge, looked again at her drawing and wondered why she had drawn a face in the privet nearest the far corner. Then, again, she wondered if it was a face at all? Certainly there were two black specks that might be eyes, and a loose black circle which suggested a mouth. She wouldn't have drawn anything so gormless and nasty-looking would she?

Making an indignant sniff she gathered up her crayons and counted them into her lap. She couldn't understand where the black one had got to. She stared back at the drawing again. She was unable to remember drawing the peculiar face. With a sigh, she put her pad down and decided to take a rest; it wasn't worth the effort of remembering.

SEVEN

WITH EYES half closed, Pippa walked slowly backwards down the aisle, towards the entrance. She was trying to imagine the place centuries ago, what it might have been like, trying to make the pictures in her mind. She pretended to be a camera, panning back from the view of the transept, sometimes holding her fingers in a square and peering through the frame. Suddenly, the feel of something solid, startled her. It pushed against her, just above the waist.

Her eyes flicked wide open, and she quickly turned.

She had walked into the edge of what looked like a cloth covered table, at the foot of the aisle. But it hadn't felt like a table.

Remembering where she was, and resisting the temptation to swear, she rubbed a bone in her spine and stared down at the 'table'. An old red sheet that she thought might have once been an altar cloth covered the entire thing, dropping down into heavy folds at the base.

After a moment's reluctance, she stretched out her hand and pulled the cover to one side.

She gasped with surprise. It wasn't a table at all. The cloth revealed instead, a sarcophagus—a stone tomb. Pippa was immediately puzzled. She looked back along the aisle.

"This is in an odd place," she whispered to herself. "Couldn't be in a more difficult spot, in fact. Why cover it up?"

She reasoned that as the congregation came and went, there would be a bottle-neck at the foot of the aisle. She tried to remember other churches that she had visited before, when her father was working. Tombs or memorials were sometimes set in the floor of the church, and more often than not located in side aisles that could be passed easily.

She shrugged her shoulders and decided to take a closer look at the thing.

The lid was an ornate pattern of fleur de lys, mixed with other kinds of leafy shapes. Most of the design had been cut into the stone a long time ago. The edges were smooth with age, but there was also a mixture of more recent styles. She twisted her head to try and see if there was any sense in the layout, but decided that there was none.

Suddenly, she realized that there were shapes in the pattern that almost resembled faces. She tilted her head again and half closed her eyes, so that her eye-lashes formed a hazy curtain. Sometimes this trick worked with puzzle pictures.

It was then that she saw something.

She opened her eyes fully. A shiver raised the hairs on the nape of her neck.

One particular face in the pattern seemed to peer out. In a real cluster of leaves, it would have been hiding, or watching. The face was either an animal's or that of a strangely deformed man's. She had noticed a monkey's and a horse's head already, but they had not bothered her as this did. This face was almost laughing, collapsed inwards on itself in some kind of grotesque way, as though it was soft wet clay.

She blinked.

It was still there and it appeared to shimmer. She wondered for a moment if this effect was perhaps from the mica crystals in the stonework?

Cautiously, she reached out to touch the engraving, to

feel the edges, just to satisfy herself that it was stone and not as soft as it looked. Then it moved.

Was its mouth opening slightly?

She immediately jerked her hand away with a small cry. She looked again.

It had gone.

She shifted her head one way and then the other, trying to see the face once more.

"Rats," she muttered. And then she realized the other reason why she had jumped. It *had* felt soft.

She looked back at the lid.

For a minute she forgot the scare, the design was brilliant, she decided, enough to cause her to imagine things. As she stepped back, she noticed a recess in the central area, dominated by two larger fleur de lys. The tie at the base of a fleur was darker than the surround, thick with dirt or other muck.

Pippa had never shaken off the treasure hunter in her after hearing her mother's stories of Abbot's gold, hidden in secret nooks and crevices, at the bottom of wells. Of valuable artifacts like the one in the famous ghost story about the strange ancient whistle and the lost East Anglian crown. Mysteries always intrigued.

She wondered if the dark patch might be a stopped-up key hole and pushed her finger into the surface. She probed, but was careful this time to notice any sensation in her fingertips. But it was only dirt and the usual deposits found on old stone.

Slowly, the muck came away. The section beneath felt smooth to the touch, but thankfully not soft. She blew into the recess, using all her fingers now, and gradually revealed a lead border. In the centre, making an elliptical shape was a piece of darkly coloured glass.

She immediately moved away, to get a better view of

how this feature was set within the rest of the top. It was almost dead centre.

Suddenly, she heard sounds from outside.

There were footsteps on gravel, heavy and determined. She had forgotten that her father had been outside. He appeared behind her and stood beneath the pointed arch of the entrance lobby.

"Sorry," he sighed. "Had to walk them to their cars. Well I didn't have to, but I thought it was diplomatic. Probably it will be the last we'll see of them for a while. I think I could put the image of a chimpanzee in that window and they wouldn't mind. It's the architect's first job for this diocese, newly qualified, and Mr Tit in a Trance was transferred here just before I got the contract."

"Mr Perkins is a sweety," Pippa insisted.

He shook his head and crossed over to her, planting a kiss on her forehead when she smiled. She glowed at seeing him, but she was still preoccupied.

"Mustn't grumble," he continued, without noticing the concern on her face. "It's thanks to Mr Perkins that I've got the work at all. His predecessors have simply ignored the job, passed over it. He said he couldn't understand why."

"Chimpanzee?" Pippa asked.

"What?" he replied, startled by her comment.

"You said something about them not bothering if . . . never mind, you said it as a joke, I think. But there are monkeys here."

"Eh?" he stared down at her.

Pippa slapped the top of the sarcophagus.

"Oh, that," he said. "Odd isn't it. Nuisance too. I had to climb over it with some scaffolding bars. I tried to find out who was buried in there. Nobody knows for sure at the diocese office. Bob Ford just shakes his head and looks wide-eyed, the same as everybody else does around here."

"Perhaps it was Master Edric? There's a small glass pane in the centre. I thought it was stained. It's certainly dark."

Farris felt for his pipe. His eyes flashed with sudden interest. Stained glass set in a tomb? But why?

Pippa brushed the remaining dirt back from the glass and proudly gestured towards her discovery with the sweep of an open palm.

Farris leaned over the top and dropped his glasses down onto the edge of his nose.

"Well, I'll be," he mumbled. "Odd."

"What is it?" Pippa asked.

"I don't know," he retorted. "Actually, I don't think I've ever seen anything like it. Ever."

He put his pipe stem into his mouth and lifted his shoulders in a lost gesture.

"I see," said Pippa, obviously put out that there was no easy answer.

"Perhaps it's a little window for whoever's in there, so that they can see out!" He burst into a laugh as he made his way over to the scaffolding.

"See out?" She repeated.

Pippa didn't join in the joke. Instead she stared back at the pane. She hadn't liked that suggestion. She hadn't liked it one bit.

EIGHT

SPROG LOOKED again, narrowing her eyes this time. She was certain that someone was waving at her again from the corner of the garden. This time her response was to stand up straight, and simply to stare back. She had been half expecting that whoever it was, would emerge from the hedge and, perhaps, introduce themselves.

She felt stupid, wondering why she had done nothing. Perhaps it wasn't anybody at all? Perhaps it had been a sheet of paper, or an effect of the sunlight? But she was sure it had been an arm.

Bella, in the meanwhile, sat beneath the willow tree, reading. She wore a summer frock and her hair was up in neat bunches, looking as though she might just be about to be invited for tea somewhere. Glancing up for a moment, she noticed Sprog standing in the middle of the lawn looking lost. A moment earlier Sprog had been playing with a sketch pad and some of her father's crayons: that was unusual for little sister.

Bella gave a deep sigh and put her book to one side.

"Sproglodyte! What is it?"

Sprog remained facing the corner of the garden with an expression of stone. Bella wondered if she had heard her. A sudden passing breeze rustled the low branches of the willow, sweeping the grass below, making it difficult for Bella to see exactly what Sprog was doing.

"Sprog!" she called again.

The branches sprang upwards.

This time Sprog turned. She had put her thumb into her mouth, and looked very faraway. Bella thought she reminded her of 'little boy lost' in a poem that she had once read. With her cropped hair and red shorts she looked the part.

"Take your thumb out of your mouth!" yelled Bella. With a groan she realized that she was going to have to go over to her.

Sprog watched Bella duck beneath the branches of the willow, and cross the lawn. Sprog felt peculiar. The sun was bright and it was a warm day, but since the wave she felt unhappy, almost sad. Sprog squinted up at the sky. The sun appeared to shimmer now with a black border. She had felt like this once before, when Daddy had explained to her about Mummy.

She looked back to the corner of the garden again. This time she hoped that there would be no figure there, that she would not see the wave.

Half way across the lawn, Bella sensed that something really was wrong. A large Jackdaw screeched overhead as it flew past, making a cry like a cackling crone. Sprog didn't seem to have heard it.

"Sprog?" Bella spoke more softly.

She rested her hand on her sister's shoulder. Sprog twisted round as though startled.

"It's me, silly. What is it?"

Sprog's eyes moved restlessly in her head, unsure how to answer.

"Come on!" Bella adopted a playful attitude.

She walked towards the corner that had held Sprog's attention, giving a glance over her shoulder to make sure that she was following. But Sprog remained stubbornly still.

"Sproglodyte!" Bella stamped her foot. "Come on I've got a surprise, Pippa found it earlier. I was saving it up till later, but I'll show it to you now if you'd like."

Sprog looked uncertain what to do, and then she

removed her thumb from her mouth. Her jaw hung open. She took a single step forward. Bella wondered how long her patience would hold out, and then she remembered her father's words, and Pippa's too. She took another deep breath and counted mentally to five.

"Come on!" She patted her leg, as if she was trying to cajole a dog into following. "Come here. What is it Pippa says, hist whist!"

Sprog began to relax. The corners of her mouth turned upwards again.

A voice in her ear suggested, *"Go on, it's safe."*

She didn't bother to turn round. As if by magic the old Sprog returned, if a little mellower.

Bella grabbed Sprog's outstretched arm and pulled her with her. They ran together, Bella almost pulling her sister into the overgrown stretch of hedge, when they reached the corner. They soon found the sundial pillar.

Sprog dug her heels into the grass and stopped just short of the pillar itself. Her face warmed with sudden interest, completely forgetting that this was the place that had troubled her so much.

She was quick to clamber round to the opposite side of the sundial, her fingers anxious to explore the feel of the thing.

"Steady on Sprog," said Bella, pleased that her sister had pulled herself out of her mood so suddenly.

"What is it Bel?" asked Sprog, now puzzling over the circular indent, in the pedestal table.

"You can tell the time with this, only the bit that is like a clock face is missing."

"It's a sundial then," Sprog concluded in a matter-of-fact voice. She was delighted with the find.

Bella felt ridiculous for a moment.

Bella was about to explain something of the principles,

in greater detail than she had intended to, when she heard a voice call out from the garden. She put her head back through the hedge and looked towards the house. A man in old clothes, wearing a peaked hat was standing outside the back door. She wasn't sure who it was at first and then a black and white bundle of fur scampered round from the side of a wooden tub, and stood beside him.

"It's Mr Ford," she muttered. "I expect he's looking for Dad."

Sprog was too busy examining the base of the sundial, to pay much attention to Bella. She played at imitating Pippa and her father, when they became engrossed in complicated exchanges of dates and opinion on 'what was what' in old buildings.

"Behave," said Bella, looking back at Sprog and wagging a finger of warning. "I'd better go and see what he's after."

Bella pushed through the hedgerow to the lawn and called out with a gesture of her arm. Sprog saw the movement of her sister's arm, through a gap in the bush. She froze, bothered by the sight of it, but then continued her play after a second or two.

"Need summin from the house," Sprog heard Bob Ford tell Bella. "Your pa said't be alright."

Within seconds, the light thump of Bella's feet as she crossed the lawn, died away, and Sprog heard the back door open and slam shut again.

She was alone.

For a moment, she half considered running after Bella. But something lingered at the back of her mind, like a thought or a suggestion that she supposed to remember. She crouched at the base of the pillar, busily removing the clumps of moss and weed.

She turned her head skywards.

The hedge and trees funneled upwards from around her. She felt closed in by it all. It was almost claustrophobic. But the sky was clear and a warm wind played with the branches of the trees, it did not seem like a day for anything untoward to happen.

The hedgerow rustled softly.

Sprog returned to her task.

The bottom of the sundial was much larger than she thought was necessary for such a short stumpy object. A layer of moss stuck fast to the base plinth. With claw fingers she scraped the stuff away. From where she crouched she could smell the mould on her fingers, tempered only by the freshness of the breeze. Her hands felt damp.

For a moment she thought that the smell was coming from elsewhere.

The bushes to the right of her suddenly shook as a paler green, which glistened as if wet, caught the sun from within the veil of leaves.

Sprog stopped and listened.

The sound of startled, sudden movement—like scurrying— assured her that it was a small animal.

She licked her lips and returned to her task.

Removing the moss had revealed a shape, cut into the stone. Black earth still clung to the pillar in places, emphasizing the outline. Sprog tried to decide what the thing was. She thought she had found a face of some kind.

She moved her head back from the image, thinking that it reminded her of something she should know well. Sprog knew a frog when she saw one, and she quickly decided that despite its fierce expression, this belonged to a frog.

She felt upwards, to a place just beneath the top of the

column, and frowned. There was a space between the top pedestal and the pillar itself.

An unexpected sense of urgency filled her: a need to perform a simple act. But to perform what?

Feeling as if she were receiving instructions from somewhere else, she stood and put both of her hands on either side of the slab, and turned the pedestal top.

The movement felt stiff at first, but then after a moment it moved, as if assisted. Stiff cogs and wheels loosened and began to engage. Turning easily again, after years of stillness.

The surrounding breeze played with her hair.

To Sprog's surprise, the sundial slid to the side, making a small arc across the ground. The base cut through the twisty knots in the undergrowth, and she heard the creaking of gears as if the earth itself might be a machine.

Something was coming.

She felt it in her bones.

A rush of air, like a foul escaping gas, shot upwards.

She cried out. A terrible smell, the same as she had smelt earlier, hit her full in the face.

NINE

BOB FORD stood at the bottom of the staircase. Bella had let him in through the garden door that led into her father's makeshift workshop.

He had paused briefly to stare at the sheets of glass, the work bench, and some designs that were pinned onto the walls with thumb tacks. Suddenly, his eyes fell on the covered easel. Bella expected him to ask her what was beneath the sheet, but instead, he moved away and mumbled, continuing instead, out into the hallway.

He looked up the staircase, arms rigidly held to his sides as though expecting instructions.

"You wanted something, Mr Ford?" Bella reminded him.

"Tha's right," he said unsmilingly. "The office rang, somethin' 'bout this new secretary feller wanting to put all the records and things into order. The Suffolk museum's got interested. Don't think they'll find anythin' that they'd want under glass, not to keep in one of their cabinets."

Bella still didn't know what it was that he was after. She looked at him with an expression that asked for more information.

Again, he looked up the stairs. He didn't seem to want to go up them.

"I need a box, see. I know it's up there, we packed it up years back. They wants the inventy."

"The what?"

"The . . ." he felt embarrassed.

"It's up there, anyhow, in a box, an inventy, you know—a list of things, they wants me to take it over when I pick up my wages."

"Oh, an inventory. Please," Bella gestured politely for him to go up, and not wishing to appear even more stupid in front of a child, he mounted the stairs.

Bob Ford climbed slowly, his head nervously shifting from side to side as he went. Bella wished he would hurry along.

"Not been up here for a long time," he almost whispered.

"But aren't you the caretaker or something?" she asked.

He glanced back, over his shoulder.

"Groundsman really. That's what the duties are, no caretakin' needed now. Place is old and nobody local'l come here. Not my job to be peekin' 'bout here. Surprised how your pa was able to rig the electric back up. I come in from time to time to look over, and a posh agency from town cleans round a bit once in a while. I don't come up here, though, up the stairs. Not here. No, not here."

He stopped on the top stair and stiffened. He had said too much.

"Not my job."

He gazed up at the ceiling, curves of old brown wallpaper, coated with thick paint, hung like folds of paper drapes.

"Not my job to get this damn box either," he added gruffly.

Bella was becoming impatient.

"Jus' let me 'ave a moment to remember where we stored the thing."

He raised his finger, to his lips, and cautiously pushed the door to his left. It creaked open with a satisfying predictability.

Bella saw an unmade bed with her father's clothes cast across the bottom. An old duvet was bundled half on to the floor.

"Your pa sleep's in here, eh?" he asked, looking at Bella with a raised eyebrow.

She nodded gently, although it was obvious that she had not been up here before. She cast a glance over the landing. She thought she heard the sound of a door, as if someone might have come in, she tilted her head to listen but decided that it was the wind. Her attention returned to Bob Ford's survey.

Bob Ford scanned the room with the same gaze of curiosity and interest, which he had shown downstairs in the workshop. There were two high backed chairs and an arm chair with loose stuffing emerging from the seat. Beside this stood a chest of drawers.

On the chest, next to a photograph of a red headed woman, was a small octagonal shaped object. It looked like a glass lantern, only the glass panels were a beautiful mosaic of colour. It had been made out of stained glass.

"This is pretty," he muttered, leaning forward to get a better look. "What is it?"

Bella froze. She didn't realise that her father still carried this about with him. She was about to reply, but checked herself. She wondered what would be the right thing to say.

Bob Ford was about to reach out and touch the object, when a commanding voice rang out from the doorway, behind them.

"Don't touch that, please!"

He almost staggered with shock, and Bella was quick to turn on her heels too, her heart beating fast. It was Pippa. Bella suddenly felt grateful that she had arrived, and ran over to her sister, fighting back a tear. She kept her back to Bob Ford and tried to speak to Pippa softly with stagily mimed lip movements.

"I'm sorry. I didn't say anything. I didn't know he still

had this, Bob Ford was asking about it."

"It's all right," Pippa whispered.

Bob Ford looked sorry for himself.

"I . . . I'm sorry Miss. I didn't mean 'arm, jus looked pretty."

"It's a lamp," said Pippa brusquely, "and it's very valuable. Dad made it."

Her eye caught Bella's.

"Can I help?" Pippa continued.

Bella watched with admiration: her sister dealt with the situation so easily.

"I got to get a box, tha's all. I . . . I am sorry if I caused . . ."

Pippa began to feel sorry for him, she had been abrupt, but he shouldn't have been so nosy. Beads of perspiration had broken out on his forehead.

Bob Ford tried to advance matters.

"Thought it might be this room, but's not. I wanned the old nursery room, one they used as a Sunday school sometime. Come on, I'll show you if you's like. I think it's further up. I'll be quick."

He left the room ahead of them.

Bella took the moment.

"Why didn't you explain?" she hissed.

"None of anyone's business but ours, not everybody thinks it's alright to carry the ashes of a person around wherever you go. Remember what Aunt Emma told us, it's Dad's way of remembering. It will just take time."

From out in the corridor they heard Bob Ford.

"It's this room, knew't was at top of stairs."

The two sisters stepped out on to the landing. Bob Ford peered from around the edge of the next door. They went in.

The room appeared much the same as the others, spacious with heavy embossed paper. There was a pile of plaster on the floor, with chunks of wooden lathe and newspaper. Pippa looked upwards and saw the beams of the loft, cobwebbed strands of dirt and rubble hung from a rough sawn limb, suspended from a rusting nail.

"Like I said, was sorta schoolroom once." He sounded tense.

Bob Ford crossed the floor to a large series of tall paneled doors. He pulled at the central handles, and swung them to one side. The interior of the cupboard was hardly an archive. But there were dusty boxes of papers on shelves, amongst rolls of card and other interesting looking items. He crouched down and reached into a bottom shelf. He looked at the boxes suspiciously.

"When he was here," he continued, "he took an occasional Bible class. Used to draw pictures of the children so's they use to say, that was why he got 'em here. More interested in making pictures with them than any tutorin'. One in partic'lar. He had 'im standing still for hours my grandmother once said. For hours. You ever tried standin' still for hours, eh?"

"He, who is he?" asked Bella. She turned from the window, she had been looking out into the garden.

"You mean Dr Barrow?" asked Pippa.

Bob Ford became still.

"Aye. Chauncey Barrow. Then it all stopped and they went away."

"Went away?" asked Pippa, becoming increasingly interested.

"Fore my time, of course." He looked stern.

"Nothin' more to say. Don't wanna spoil your holiday."

Suddenly, he made a noise of triumph and yanked at something far back on the shelf.

"This'll be him I think, what we're after, bloody Mr Perkins comin' and stirring everythin' up."

He pulled himself up on to his haunches and tucked a brown cardboard box under his arm.

Pippa noticed that Bella was now very occupied looking at something outside. A brown, stained net curtain hung across the two large panes. She had tucked the curtain to one side and was peering through a section of glass that she had only just wiped with her palm.

"You can see the back garden," she said.

"Sprog!" Pippa exclaimed, she had forgotten about her sister. "I had come back to check on her."

"It's all right, I was just looking myself. You can just see her, she's out there, playing with the sundial I think."

Bob Ford's head shot round, eyes wide, his mouth downturned.

He gave an involuntary groan. Pippa looked back at him. He seemed unwell. His forehead glistened, brighter than before.

"Mr Ford, are you all right?" she asked.

TEN

THE STENCH almost bowled Sprog over. As she stumbled to one side, her foot caught a small rock, which she kicked in the direction of the sundial. She heard an echoing crash, as though the rock was falling into a shaft and bouncing against the sides in its descent.

Sprog quickly regained her balance. The smell had shot out of the ground like an angry discharge of steam, but it had continued upwards and away. The summery smells of leaf and sweet scented flowers were soon recovered.

Cautiously, she edged forwards to the pillar.

The base had slid to one side to reveal a hole, lined with circular cobble-stones. She looked into the darkness. It went down a long way, but as her eyes adjusted, she saw that the hole also appeared to widen, further down.

Sprog crept nearer, leaning over the edge this time.

There was still a smell, but it was more like gas from a stagnant pond. She heard something move too, a stir of water, followed by a plopping sound as if something had emerged from water. A call followed, not unlike a frog or toad's croak, but lower and wetter somehow.

She shifted forwards on her stomach to get even closer. It was difficult to see clearly, the hedge cast its shadow across the opening. She thought that just below, cut into the side, were small steps.

For a moment she wondered what they could be for.

Gradually, the structure became clearer. The walls glistened, and she now noticed patches of a thick furry covering that clung to the cobble stones like a strange skin.

Sprog felt behind her for another stone and dropped it

into the shaft.

This time, the echo of its descent as it hit the sides of the shaft was unmistakable, and after a moment there came a full plopping ring, contained and exact but far louder than the earlier sound.

"Water, thought so," mumbled Sprog to herself, becoming increasingly fascinated with her find. Pippa had always gone on about how she would love to find a secret passage or something like it in an old abbey, or some such place. Now Sprog had found a special secret all on her own. Pippa would be pleased.

She looked over the edge again.

There was a movement below her: had some mould or fungus just fallen away from the side? It had flapped in a funny way, almost reminding her of the wave that she thought she had seen earlier.

A softer echo followed, an animal noise again.

"Hallo!" Sprog called down into the darkness.

She giggled as her voice echoed back.

"Lo, lo . . ." came the echo.

"Go on, ask," a voice came, gently in her ear.

"Is anyone there?" she called out.

Another voice came back to her. She was sure it was a frog, it gurgled. Sprog's heart thumped with excitement.

She heard a rustling, like the patter of tiny feet on wet leaves.

"Froggy!"

The rustling moved closer. She so wanted to meet him.

"Let's see you then, please," she asked.

The thud of her heartbeat filled her ears, something was coming, suddenly she pulled her head back.

A blackness, like the deepest of shadows rushed up towards her, threatening to catch her in an awful embrace. Sprog called out and rolled to the side. It was as though a cloak had been thrown in her face. A momentary blast, like a sudden wind, charged about her and then, almost as suddenly, a thick silence fell.

Sprog found herself on her back, looking up at the clouds. They had arranged themselves into a face, heavy with drooping folds of skin. The face stared down at her for a few moments, and then heaved and shifted into motion. The clouds separated, like pulled wooly strands and sped onwards in total silence, becoming fleeting spirits. Their shadowy shapes moved across her. The warmth from the sun had lifted, and she felt a chill.

Sprog got to her feet and looked about, the taste had gone out of the day. A pair of birds in a nearby tree suddenly sounded angry, squawking like a pair of fighting crows. The hedges shuffled their branches and a nettle scratched across her arm, causing her to smart. She wondered what she should do.

Her instinct was to 'shut up the box.'

Not wanting to get into trouble, she moved towards the sundial and tried to turn the plinth again. It was easier this time, it had been made to open and shut almost at a touch. The pillar rolled back into place, like a well-used door. It was her secret, for the holiday.

She smiled with satisfaction, almost untouched by the dark side of her discovery, and thought that she should go and find Bella.

BELLA TURNED sharply towards Pippa. She hoped for an explanation as to why an awful shudder had rippled through her body. It had arrived with the rise of the wind outside. But the look on her sister's face told her that she had experienced the same feeling, and that she had no answer.

The wind slapped against the window pane, making

Bella jerk her head back, as though the slap had been across her own face.

The floorboards of the room creaked, and there was a scurrying below, as if a nest of rats had been disturbed. Board nails twisted and eased their way upwards, the door groaned wider on its hinges.

Bob Ford reached out and supported himself against the cupboard door. He simply stared directly ahead, his eyes almost sightless and his face without colour. Pippa could hear his breathing. He looked over at Bella. His bottom lip trembled as though he was about to speak, but instead, he gripped the box more firmly beneath his arm and hurried out of the room.

The two girls watched him leave in silence, hearing clearly the scuff of his boots on the edge of the stairs.

As he opened the back door the whimpering of his dog leaked into the house. Something had clearly terrified the animal, almost as much as Bob Ford.

ELEVEN

FARRIS SAT at the kitchen table with his arm outstretched in front of him. It helped the pain. There had been a peculiar dull ache in his hand, which had crept up on him during the day. By early afternoon he had dropped his pliers for the seventh or eighth time, he didn't know which, and it was then that he noticed how blue and swollen his fingers had become.

He felt unwell too, but was managing to retain something of his spirits for the sake of the girls. His condition had cast gloom over the rest of the day. Returning to the Grange through the trees, the sunset had looked angry. The summer sky in these parts could be startling, but this evening it was muddied, contaminated.

He had lingered for a moment before entering the Grange. The place looked hollow and fragile like a dead shell, the spires and gables unnatural growths on a decaying body.

The girls had noticed a difference when they met in the kitchen. Corners harboured secrets. Silent moments lingered. Footsteps echoed long after footfall. Farris put it down to his mood.

After Pippa had turned down the heat on the grill, she sat by her father and re-inspected his hand. The ends of two of his fingers had gone black. He looked sorry for himself.

Sprog had been very quiet, having found some jam jars beneath the sink. She was busily tying some garden twine around their necks to make handles.

Bella crossed to the table and joined in with Pippa's inspection of their father's hand. She pulled a face and returned to the sink.

"Is it as bad as it looks?" asked Pippa, pulling a concerned expression that echoed Bella's.

"It just aches," Farris complained, displaying a trace of irritation, "right up to the elbow joint too."

"Do you think it's infected? Did you cut yourself or something?"

Farris sighed and pulled his arm away, deciding that perhaps it might be better to let it enjoy a lower profile with Sprog about. He leaned forward and spoke quietly.

"I think I know where it's come from, but don't ask me to explain it." He gestured with his finger, for her to move closer.

Pippa tilted her head towards him.

"That bloody sundial top, remember? I scraped away some moss didn't I? Perhaps it's poisonous, it did get under my nail after all."

She became thoughtful again, wondering if the explanation sounded plausible.

"Well that's what I think anyhow," he continued, without waiting for her comment. "I think its easing off now, it's just this strange numbness. It's come at a choice time too, what with that window and all."

"Ah!" said Pippa, remembering. "You never did finish explaining that to me. There's time. Dinner won't be ready just yet."

He leaned back in his chair.

Sprog suddenly turned from the sink, proudly holding three jam jars from string loops.

Pippa gave her father a knowing look and even Bella stopped what she was doing for a second.

"Can I go out and play please?" asked Sprog very politely. "It's gloomy in here."

Farris agreed, wearily.

"Don't go near the pond," Bella warned, "I promised we could play there tomorrow," then she added, "perhaps".

"No. I won't, I'm just going to be in the garden," Sprog stared innocently.

"She's up to something," mumbled Pippa. "Sproglodyte, why the jam jars then?"

"Froggies!" the gap toothed smile reappeared.

"Let her go," he said, with a huge sigh. "She can't get into much trouble. Promise to come in the minute Pippa calls out for dinner, right?"

Sprog nodded, it was almost a bow, and went out into the hallway.

"What was the meeting about then?" Pippa continued, trying to change the subject, to brighten matters.

Farris tapped his fingers on a cardboard folder, he seemed faintly amused by something.

"You recall that central window—the large one, or rather the empty space?"

"Yes?"

"Well, it's just that I'm not certain if the scene is biblical or not. I think it's a single figure."

"How do you know that?"

"Partly guessing, and judging from some bits and pieces that were left at the edges, it may be a portrait. There are little vignettes in the border panes. I can measure something of the style from those. Incidentally, I think it's more likely to be the work of the assistant."

"So," said Pippa with a trace of impatience, "why did you have to see Mr Perkins and the suit?"

"I just needed the okay to use my imagination, that's all. Like I told you, I don't think our Mr Perkins really minds what goes in there. The architect feller's a bit of a waste of time."

He flexed his fingers and yawned.

"I did get a useful suggestion from Mr Perkins though."

"I think they're all acting strange out here," said Pippa, suddenly side-tracking.

"Mr Perkins isn't a local," said Farris.

"What about that Mr Ford? He was behaving really oddly upstairs today."

Farris went quiet.

"I . . . I don't think he likes it in here," said Farris, lowering his voice. "He told me, when I first arrived, that he played here when he was a boy. You know kids, the place got itself a reputation."

Bella turned around, her face hoped for a story.

"Not—the bad house?"

Farris tried to laugh.

"Well . . . he wouldn't say. I don't think I know of an old house that hasn't got some kind of 'history'. It comes with the age you know. I think our Dr Chauncey Barrow had a bit of a reputation."

"He used to make his Bible class children be models," chirped in Bella.

"What?"

"Mr Ford told us. He made drawings of them, apparently."

"Ah." Farris' face lit up, as though a piece of a puzzle had suddenly fallen into place.

"What is it?" Pippa asked, seeing his expression.

"It's just that many faces in his stained glass pieces do look rather young. I had trouble with some scenes, for that reason. You know, trying to decide what the picture was depicting. I think you've just given me a possible answer, young lady."

Bella looked suitably smug and returned to her duties, humming something tuneless.

Pippa had an idea.

"There might be more answers in the boxes upstairs," she suggested.

"How do you mean?"

"Well there's a cupboard full of stuff from the old Sunday school class in one of the rooms. Mr Ford had to collect a box for the diocese office. In fact, I imagine that there could be valuable stuff there. I can't believe it's all been left, for just anyone to take. Mr Ford wanted the inventy."

Farris stretched out his legs.

"The what?"

"He meant inventory."

Farris nodded.

"Oh, oh, of course. I see your point though about it being worth something. The stuff could be over a hundred years old. I've come across stranger in old places, though. Who's going to take packets of old papers and things? It's computers and televisions that thieves go looking for."

"I suppose so," agreed Pippa. "Anyhow, even if that Mr Perkins does act like a bit of a wally, he's concerned enough to try to put a collection together. At least I think that's what he's up to."

"Better do it before Mr Perkins has the lot removed then. I don't know if you'll find anything to help me."

He stretched out his arm again. It was obviously still bothering him. "I meant to ask you. How'd you like a trip to Bury, to look at the cathedral there? It isn't very far."

Pippa loved cathedrals, her face showed positive interest. Bella beamed with support.

"Well, Mr Perkins told me that one of the Chauncey Barrow windows, is there. It was given to the cathedral after St Mary's went into disuse. Probably by some enterprising previous official I suppose. It's in better condition than these, intact too. I couldn't have done my homework properly, I had no idea about it. The way the history of this place falls together would have made a jigsaw easier work."

"Can we go and look now?" asked Bella. "At the boxes upstairs, I mean?"

"Dinner's going to be late," said Pippa with a sigh. "We're running at half power."

Farris welcomed the opportunity for a break. He began to get up from his chair, the room was falling into gloom now.

"I think I'll just lie down for a bit," he said quietly.

"I'll call you for dinner, yes?" Pippa helped him to his feet.

"Wouldn't miss that for the world. The arm's not so bad now, I'm just very tired, that's all. Whatever this thing is, it seems to have knocked the stuffing out of me."

He ambled towards the door and out into the hallway. Pippa and Bella heard him climb the stairs with slow, cautiously taken steps. He had suddenly aged.

TWELVE

SPROG MOVED the sundial without any hesitation. It was as easy as opening a door. As before, there was a gassy smell, but this time there was no alarming rush, the odour wafted gently from the opening instead. The smell lasted only for seconds, and then disappeared, replaced by the cool evening smells of night blossom and lavender.

Behind her, Sprog heard the flitting and squeak of small bats as they circled the perimeter of the garden. The moon was rising and soon night would fall.

She looked down into the opening, and whispered.

"Froggy, are you there?"

A soft watery plop echoed upwards.

"Come, come follow," came a voice inside her head.

She felt a little afraid.

Sprog swung her legs over the side of the hole and tried to find the top step with her foot. The edge of the stone was wet and slippery, as if coated with mould or fungus. The surface shone. As she slowly let her full weight down on to the surface, she thought it felt like sponge.

She turned and reached for one of her jam jars, which she had left by the side of the pillar.

Something moved on a lower step, it was either another piece of moss falling away from the wall, or a gesture from someone. But that was a silly idea, how could that be?

A prickly sensation, rippled through her body like an emerging riptide.

"I'm here, shall we play?"

It was an invitation.

Her lips parted.
She whispered back, "I'm coming to get you . . ."

THIRTEEN

AFTER MAKING certain that Bella had everything to hand, to finish preparing dinner, Pippa went quietly upstairs to check that her father was all right. She was now beginning to worry, not just about his uncharacteristically agitated behaviour, but at how easily he seemed to be wearing himself down.

She stopped at the top of the stairs and listened. The door to his room was ajar and he was stretched out on the top of the bed. It hadn't taken Farris long to fall asleep. The duvet was bunched up into an untidy bundle at the bottom of the bed, part of it draped down onto the floor. A small table lamp glowed on the dresser, beside her mother's urn. The half-light picked up the colour in the glass, making the urn even more like an exotic eastern lantern.

Pippa glanced upwards at the lonely dusty bulb, which hung from a makeshift flex, above the landing. She longed for there to be more light in the house. The wiring was old fashioned, it barely worked at all and there was a generator to be used as a booster for cooking. She wished Dad had brought a supply of brighter bulbs; the brown paper and the muddy-coloured varnishing didn't help the depressing atmosphere. Occasional dips in the supply lowered the light unexpectedly at times. Now, she understood why he had stocked up with candles.

Assured that her father was dozing safely, she wondered whether she could find any of the old papers in the schoolroom. It suddenly occurred to her that there might not be any electric light in there. She looked back into her father's bedroom and had an idea. There were a couple of squat-looking candles fixed on to a small plate, beside the lamp.

Stepping slowly, so as not to wake him, she squeezed through the opening in the doorway and crossed to the dresser.

She could see him better now, his face was creased, as though he was in pain. His lip turned upwards like a dreaming dog's, and he made little murmuring noises in his sleep.

She decided to let him to sleep on, and reached for the candles, pausing to stare at the urn. It really was a work of art, possibly one of her father's best pieces. She felt sorry that the achievement was linked with sadness. She wished that he would leave it somewhere, and allow the past to become the past. Her friend at school had told her it was a 'morbid' idea, but had later apologized about the remark. She had not meant to sound unkind, although Pippa couldn't help thinking she might be right.

The silver of the moon rose above the trees in the distance, casting a satin lustre glow through the window. The sky appeared reluctant to turn to night. The remains of the day shimmered beneath the evening.

She turned to look back at the room. Her father's apron hung from a hook on the edge of the dresser. She felt in the pocket and found his pipe, and then she discovered the matches. Putting the box in her pocket she took the saucer of candles. With a final glance towards her father, she tiptoed across to the doorway and out of the room.

She became very conscious of the creaking of the boards, as she walked along the landing. An old rug lay across several loose planks, but still the sound reverberated, like the prised lid of a wooden box.

Suddenly, to her surprise, she heard the cry of a young

child. It sounded far away.

"Sprog?" she said, not at all certain that it was her sister. "Is that you, whatever's wrong?"

The cry seemed to soften and acquire a faint echo that gave it a sudden ethereal quality.

"Who. . . is it?" whispered Pippa. "Where are you?"

It occurred to her that she did not really know where the sound was coming from. She stood very still for a moment and listened carefully.

The cries hardened, now they came like tiny sharply-taken breaths.

An animal, maybe a bat, squeaked outside. It seemed to fly over the roof. She looked upwards, wondering if that was what she had heard, and not a child. Then the cry became louder. This time the location was unmistakable. The pitiful sighs had turned to low sobs, and they came from the schoolroom.

"Sproglodyte?"

Pippa felt strangely reluctant to continue along the landing.

The sobbing increased, it was clearer now. The owner of the voice was obviously in distress. Pippa glanced behind her, could anyone else hear it, would it wake her father?

Suddenly, she heard her father call. His voice sounded deeper than usual—almost a growl, and he spoke in short meaningless sentences. His voice alternately rose and fell with tiny whimpers, he was clearly having a nightmare.

The crying from the schoolroom turned to a moan, awful and desperate. Pippa seemed surrounded by the sounds of fear. A claw squeezed her heart.

The schoolroom voice became desperate.

"Oh my God, the schoolroom," she whispered.

Something was happening in there.

"Who is it?" she called out, and moved cautiously down the landing.

"Sprog, it is you isn't it?"

She pushed the schoolroom door open; a small voice screamed as she did so. It seemed to descend below the floor as though its owner had been thrown into a deep space. The echo decayed abruptly.

She swallowed a mouthful of air as she realized that nobody was there, and remembered with abrupt clarity that Sprog was outside. At the same time, she heard the shriek of an adult.

"Dad!" she shouted.

She turned on her heels and ran back along the landing. Through the banister rails she saw Bella, rushing up the flight of stairs from below, her face ashen.

The door was still ajar. As she entered the room her father sat bolt upright. His face was fierce and huge in the glow of the light. He made quick movements with his arm, as though trying to rip through an invisible curtain in front of him. Pippa thought he held something in his hand, which was clenched into a fist.

She ran to the bedside and tried to hold his arm still. His wide eyes saw nothing.

He shouted out a name which Pippa was unable to catch.

Farris stared into Pippa's face. For a moment he appeared confused as though woken from a trance. His body became tense. Something terrible had surfaced.

Bella trembled in the doorway, nervous and uncertain what she should do next.

After a moment Farris' eyes showed that he recognized them. He almost collapsed back on to the pillow with relief.

"Dad?" said Pippa gently, "you were dreaming. What

was it?"

Pearls of perspiration glistened on his forehead.

"Sprog . . ." he muttered between swallows. "Oh God, Sprog. I dreamt . . . I dreamt I did something awful . . . terrible . . . to . . . to . . ."

Anxiety welled up in his face, as he realized that there were only the two of them standing in the room.

"Sprog!" he shouted. "Where, where is Sprog?"

He kicked the cover away from his feet and swung his legs around. He almost fell as he stumbled drunkenly across the room to the doorway.

Pushing past Bella he made for the landing and they heard the latch click of a downstairs' door. The two girls followed.

He froze halfway down the stairs.

The dark haze of the wallpaper appeared to ripple, light fell awkwardly.

Sprog stood in the hallway, she looked disheveled and grubby with blotches of green smeared about her face. From her upheld hand there hung a jam jar. She held it up for everyone to see, proud of her possession. It was full of murky water, slithers of weed, stuck around the mouth of the jar, where the string was tied. The light caught silver specks, which floated slowly to the bottom of the water.

"See my jar?" said Sprog, an artful grin creeping across her face. "I caught a froggy, only one of his little ones. But it escaped."

Farris caught something else in his daughter's eyes. It was a certain look, a glint in her eyes, which he would have preferred not to have seen.

FOURTEEN

PIPPA AWOKE several times during the night, tossed awake by the sudden roll of her head, or the kick of her leg against the bed clothes. Each time it became more difficult to return to sleep, and at one point she thought that Bella or Sprog might be equally restless.

She remembered waking with a start and seeing somebody sitting upright, across the room. The figure was just a shape in the silver-grey of the moonlight, and appeared to be watching or listening. Finally, she had softly said 'go back to sleep' and the shape had collapsed back into the bed clothes. She had supposed it was Sprog. Bella was bigger.

For a long while she stared at the ceiling of the room, half listening for sounds from upstairs. All was quiet and still, apart from the usual murmurings, common in old country houses.

It was a little before dawn that the dream came.

Pippa found herself drifting along the upstairs landing, but it seemed that she was approaching the stairs from the far end of the passage. Each door opened slowly, but the wrong way—outwards, as if she were somehow being invited or challenged to enter.

From this approach, the schoolroom was on the right. Here, a bare arm stretched out from behind the door-frame. The flesh was translucent, the fingers slender and very pale.

She had no control over her movement. She felt as though she were continuing forward in a strange kind of ecstasy of slow motion, as though blown along by a breeze.

As she neared the door a single finger beckoned to her, its nail was long, almost to a point, like a knife. For a moment she stood outside, as the hand withdrew. Within the room a voice, old, wet and breathless could barely be heard.

Pippa listened, she could not help herself.

"Turn, turn pretty one. That's my lovely, that's my treasure. Turn this way first, and then that. Oh, what delight, you fill my heart with such gladness. Can you dance? Just a step perhaps? Maybe if I clap my hands like this, you will find it easier? Or perhaps, like this?

"Oh, too fast, too fast, my poor boy, my dear. Did I make you gad and tumble there, in such an ungainly fashion? It's so, so, unfair of me. Steady now. Twirl, twirl, that's the way my pretty, that's the way."

A small voice struggled to reply. Pippa could not hear what it said. The wet voice rasped sharply, in response.

"What's that you say? You're tired? No matter. Up now, on your pretty toes, to make you much taller, to make your swan neck grow. Raise your chin a little more. Such a pretty neck, your finest feature I should say. Up my dear. Now turn a little to the right, now twist to the left. The light! My child, my child, mind the light—this is your better side. Young fool, have you no soul?

"Turn, now.

"Do as I say, please.

"Do it."

Pippa's throat tightened. A sense of dread began to stir at the pit of her stomach. The voice became harder.

"Stretch up, hold your chin. Hold as I say. That's it."

A long sigh followed.

"Oh, I grow giddy from your beauty."

The voice became hard, crueler than barbed wire.

"Listen to me now, listen very carefully. Don't move,

not a single muscle. Can you hear your heart beat? Such a strong heart. I can see the tiny pulse in your neck, just there, beckoning to me almost. Be still!"

Pippa's own heart beat thundered in her ears.

"Young fool! Damn you, damn your soul!

"Be still!—Don't make me rage, I warn you now. Curse your eyes. Be as still as grave bones, as silent as a shroud. Hear me well, if I so much as see the air stir before your pretty lips, you'll never take breath again.

"Ahhh!"

"That's better, much better.

"I can watch you. We'll soon have your fine form captured here by my friend. Stand as you are, there are many more hours till morning, aren't there?

"Aren't there? Hist whist."

A laugh followed, sour and empty.

Pippa could not remember passing through the doorway, the scene melted like the rippling of a reflection in water. A young boy stood before her, scruffily dressed in a white ragged shirt, with a grey waistcoat unbuttoned at the front. The collar, and the upper part of his shirt, had been turned down: tucked in to reveal the sweep of his neck, down to his shoulders. The boy either stood on a chair or a stool, she could not tell which.

She wondered for a moment if he was showing her something, a mark on his shoulder or neck perhaps? He was strikingly beautiful, with very dark brown hair and a pale and innocent face. She kept wondering what it was that he was doing, then something about his stance struck her like a blow. Not only could she now see that he was trembling visibly, but the eyes held terror, perhaps the most terrible she thought she had ever seen.

Whatever it was that guided her, now twisted her around as though she might be inspecting the boy. His eyes followed her as she turned, the helpless look of fear seemed to deepen.

Again, the scene rippled and re-appeared as though set in the distance. She could see more clearly now, he stood on a stool.

A huddled thing, like an old man, shifted awkwardly in a far corner. It was cloaked in a garment that reminded her of a huge riding hood. But the hood flexed as though the creature it contained was uncomfortable, swallowing light as it moved. It was this that bothered the boy, and Pippa.

Did she see a hand from within the blackness, or was it a talon, like a large bird's? It had been puffy with scales like a lizard's. Whatever the figure was, it was watching the boy and making notes, or performing something that required observation.

She became aware that there was somebody else in the room. She saw him out of the corner of her eye, and he seemed to be waiting. Formally dressed, the figure was staring at the boy.

"Capture," said the figure.

She tried to see who it was, but the scene dissolved again.

Pippa awoke slowly, without the sudden shock that usually comes with bad dreams. The dawn chorus of birds brought her round. The morning shone through the window with an alarming brightness. Her sense of time had collapsed.

Her father stood in the doorway with a struggling smile and a tray in his hands. She tried to return the pleasant expression, but felt low spirited, almost miserable.

The other two awoke more quickly.

As her father reached down to give Sprog a morning

kiss, she realized that her sister's beds were to the right of hers. They were not directly in front.

She wondered who or what it was that she had told to go back to sleep in the middle of the night.

FIFTEEN

KIT FARRIS acted as though nothing untoward had happened the previous night. Pippa and Bella exchanged looks across the table. Bella was becoming increasingly astute in reading her older sister and remained silent, allowing Pippa to take any lead, if there was to be a discussion.

Bella wondered if his silence was for Sprog's benefit. Her father had almost smothered Sprog with attention, cleaning her up, at the sink, whilst she and Pippa managed to save the evening meal. No questions were asked, or reprimand given for her having returned home in such a state. "A bad dream," was her father's explanation for crying out in his sleep.

Pippa had no explanation at all for her own experience.

She waited patiently whilst Sprog hurried through her toast. Sprog's eyes kept flitting across to the sink, where her jam jar of stagnant water stood.

"I'm going out to play, Daddy," she declared suddenly, jumping down from the table.

She crossed to the sink and reached for her jar.

""I'm going to find froggies, there's a nice big one here. I call him Mister Damp, 'cos he's all wet and shiny. He's got a floppy head that's all squashed and he keeps laughing."

Pippa looked up. The imaginary friend sounded awful.

"No," said Farris firmly. "No playing in ponds."

"Good for you, Dad," said Pippa to herself.

"I told you that the pond is out of bounds, unless you have your sisters with you and . . ."

"Didn't go in the pond," replied Sprog sulkily.

"All right then, but you must have gone somewhere damn well like it to have got in such a mess. Where then, young madam?"

Sprog became coy.

"Secret," she muttered. "Mister Damp told me that I mustn't tell."

Pippa was about to protest when her father held up his hand to her.

"Wait a minute. If Sprog has a secret then that's fair enough, but keep away from this place for now, all right? Agree and we won't pry."

Sprog thought about this for a moment and then nodded sagely. She kept crossed fingers behind her back.

"Tell you what," he continued, "in my workroom, there's some large sheets of sketching paper. Take yourself off and design a stained glass window for me. Stay there. We'll be in soon, it looks like I'll be in that room quite a bit today. Catching up to do."

Sprog appeared well pleased with this suggestion and ran to the door. She hesitated before opening it and returned, dashing across to the sink. She took her jam jar down, the sudden movement agitated the silvery flecks from the bottom of the water.

"Sprog!" shouted Bella.

"Can I paint?" asked Sprog, looking at her father.

"Yes . . . of course, why?"

Sprog sniffed at Bella and held the jar higher.

"Then the water is for my brushes of course, thank you," she snootily explained.

Nose held high, she left.

"Let her have her secrets, everybody has some. I should know." Farris poured out some more tea. Pippa was not sure about this. She harboured doubts about such an 'easy-going' attitude. Then Farris added, "do you know where it was she went?"

"She was playing around the sundial, but she wouldn't have got in that state there," said Bella.

Pippa shrugged and Farris shrugged in return.

"You're in a good mood," Pippa ventured.

"I think it's just because I felt so awful last night. You're a wonder to have got on with the dinner."

Bella coughed loudly.

"You too," he added.

Pippa looked across at his hand, it was almost back to its proper colour.

"Oh, that's fine," he noticed her quick inspection.

"I had a strange dream during the night," she suddenly announced.

"I dreamt last night as well," he replied casually, "but I'm damned if I can remember what. Yesterday is like a haze. I think I had a touch of fever."

"It wasn't the dream that scared me, so much. Not at first," Pippa tried to explain. "I heard a voice. It wasn't the first time either."

"Voice?" Farris began to fidget. He seemed uncomfortable with the topic. Bella cocked her head to one side, she didn't know anything of this.

"I thought it was Sprog. In a funny kind of way the voice wasn't unlike hers. I heard it the first night, I thought you did too, and again last night just before you cried out. When you were having that nap." She darted a questioning look towards Bella. "You heard it, didn't you? You were half way up the stairs."

"That was because of Dad, I thought he shouted to me. I didn't hear anything else."

Pippa went silent. The other pair looked at one another.

"Perhaps I confused things," she mused.

Her father became very quiet, glancing down at the table cloth as though searching for something to say, for a minute he looked completely lost. Pippa thought he was about to volunteer new information when he coughed and rose to his feet instead.

He went to lift his plate, when suddenly he flexed his fingers. He stretched them outwards, trying to part them as he did so.

"Damn it!"

Bella leaned towards him. He dismissed the outburst with a wave.

"Still sore," he grumbled.

"We can help," chirped Pippa, deciding there had been enough gloom and solemnity.

The urgent ringing of a telephone, startled the girls. It came from the hallway. Pippa and Bella looked at one another. It was the first time they had heard it.

"Answer it Pippa, would you?" Farris muttered. "It's out in the hallway on an orange crate."

Pippa made her way to the hall and saw an old black telephone, almost hidden within the shadow-filled corner by the door.

She picked up the receiver.

"Hallo? Kit Farris' daughter speaking," she smiled down the phone.

She recognized the voice at the other end. It was Mr Perkins. He had lost his nervous titter, but retained the sing-song character.

"No need to bother Dad," he suggested. "You're well up on these things too, eh, eh. I can tell you, and then you can tell him. I rang because I thought you'd be interested in something that I've discovered. Your dad asked to be kept in touch."

"What is it, Mr Perkins?" Pippa asked, trying to pull

him to the point.

"It's only that I found out more about our site there, and Master Edric. The venerable archdeacon helped, turns out we have some records ourselves, mmm, down in London. Firstly, I was amazed to discover that charcoal burners used that site. Mmm, really. I'm going back a long way now."

"Yes?" said Pippa, not understanding the significance.

"Well, you see they had problems, troubles. Quite well documented. Mmm. You see, it's got a strange history, shall we say. The men were bothered by mischievous spirits, place was known for it. Local people in the villages all had a sorry time with demons and goodness knows what. Ghost stories, eh?"

He recounted the story with unmistakable relish. Pippa listened with growing interest.

"It was thought that bringing an abbey to the place would make the site holy and the spirits would leave. That was how the monk's quarter came into being. I didn't know that, you know. It's fascinating, eh? Mmm."

"You've been busy Mr Perkins," said Pippa, thoughtfully.

"The other thing concerns Master Edric," he continued. "Remember we were talking about him. We cannot be absolutely certain, but it's a good bet that Edric was buried in that stone tomb in the church. It's unmarked you see. Mmm."

"We wondered about that," said Pippa.

"Yes, well, there we are. Do you know we have proof that he made it himself? Fancy that. It wasn't his final resting place though. No. They pulled him out of there a bit sharpish. Mmm. Our man in London thinks he was probably just re-buried in waste ground, or put in a pit somewhere."

"Why did they . . ."

"Pull him out? I'm not sure yet. I'm going to try to get to the bottom of the story. It was something that he had done, his accuser was a certain Master Hugo. He claimed that he had been cursed, bewitched by Edric. Sounds like the usual medieval obsession to me, the previous history of the place and so on, perhaps? Mmm. I'll get in touch when I learn some more."

Pippa was fascinated.

"Oh, I nearly forgot," he added. "This is fun. This Hugo was visited each night and tormented by Edric's familiars—you know like witch's cats? Only it wasn't cats with Edric. Oh no, not at all. Not even a decent Hob Goblin."

"What kind of creature was it then?" asked Pippa.

There was silence for a moment, followed by a hint of a giggle.

"Guess. Mmm."

"I've no idea, Mr Perkins."

"Go on, you'll never believe it, your sister would love it, I think.!"

He giggled again.

Pippa rolled her eyes upwards.

"I'm in a bit of a hurry, Mr Perkins."

Another silence followed.

"We think they may have been . . . toads."

PIPPA JOINED the others in the workshop, and found them busily involved in various tasks. Sprog had her head down in the corner, drawing or colouring in something on a large sheet of paper.

Farris decided that he would try and keep Sprog on a short rein for a little while. He thought it prudent to give Bella something that would pull her into the work spirit of the place. She was already sorting through a mixed box of smaller sections of coloured glass, and laying them out on a sheet of felt.

Farris had removed the sheet from the mysterious window. It stood prominently, on an easel. He was busy twisting the wrist of his afflicted hand, trying to get the circulation moving through his fingers.

Pippa was about to call over to him, when she saw a woman's face peer through the garden window. The woman moved across to the garden door. She was small and slender, attractive with blonde hair tied back in a band; Pippa thought she looked about thirty. The woman tapped on the glass.

Farris looked up, wondering where the sound had come from. He turned round in time to see her wave.

"Goodness, it's Sarah," he said.

Pippa noticed his face dissolve from surprise to pleasure, as he hurried to let her in.

Bella glanced up at her sister, but Pippa remained still, quietly taking note. Farris opened the door, just a little way at first, and leaned through. Pippa was unable to see why he had done this, and what it was that they were doing. She supposed he might be giving the visitor a quick rundown on his new workshop colleagues. Bella thought he might be giving her a kiss.

After a few seconds he opened the door wide, and the woman stepped in with a smile.

Pippa walked over to where Bella was standing, and whispered in her ear.

"Do you think this is Dad's new found 'friend'?"

Bella giggled.

"Dad with a girlfriend!"

"Girls," Farris announced, "I'd like you to meet Sarah Prestwood. Without her, I couldn't be getting on here."

"I let your dad use my kiln," she quietly explained.

Her voice sounded kind: it had warmth, but it also had a strength that engaged attention.

Pippa decided that she was very attractive.

"You're a potter," said Pippa, holding out her hand in greeting.

"That's right, my fame goes before me, yes?"

Bella stepped forward, seeing that Pippa had given her initial approval. She held out her hand for Sarah to shake.

Sarah Prestwood laughed at their formality, and Farris almost looked embarrassed. She searched out the corner behind, where the industrious Sprog, who was still working in a huddle, had managed to get some gold and red stain across her face.

"And who is this?" she asked, moving away from the group towards Sprog.

"That's Stephanie," said Farris, raising his voice so that Sprog might hear, and perhaps stop what she was doing.

"It's Sprog actually," Pippa explained, not meaning to sound as haughty as she did. "I mean, that's the silly name we call her," she added, to lighten the moment.

Sprog's head remained down.

Farris caught up with Sarah and lowered his voice.

"I told you about Sprog, bit strange. Not exactly hyperactive, but has a . . . well it's a sort of individuality . . . a . . ."

He broke off, feeling that he was making a mess of the explanation.

"Sprog's eccentric," said Pippa with a casual sniff.

Farris made a face of agreement, he thought he could go along with that.

"Damn right I am," Sprog said, unexpectedly looking up.

Sarah stifled her cry of surprise.

Then Pippa saw what Sprog had been doing.

"Sproglodyte!" she shouted. "Oh no!"

Sprog blinked innocently.

Farris looked down at his work area and groaned. He lifted his hands, and buried his face into cupped palms.

She had been painting her design using one of her father's best china hair brushes, and his specially mixed stain that he had prepared for work on the window.

Pippa carefully placed the brushes to one side. She crumpled up her nose in disgust when she realized that Sprog had even used her jam jar of pond water to rinse the brushes.

Sarah Prestwood put her hand in front of her mouth, her warm eyes showed that she had difficulty in suppressing laughter.

"It's not too bad," said Pippa, trying to save something of Sprog's tarnished image.

"But it's so pretty," said Sarah, turning the paper round for a better view.

Sprog beamed with pride.

"What is it?" asked Farris, almost beneath his breath.

"Anyone can see that it's a heart, isn't that right?" said Sarah, giving Sprog's shoulder a gentle squeeze.

Sprog displayed the gap-toothed grin. She twisted her head round to obtain a better view of her new-found champion.

"Can we make a stained glass from it, can we Daddy?"

"We'll see," said Farris, grudgingly.

"You did tell Sprog to make herself a design," Pippa said with a half-smile. She looked down her nose as she re-arranged Sprog's things on another surface.

"They're all against me!" sighed Farris.

Sprog's attention was suddenly taken with a bright shiny piece of orange glass. It hung from a beaded necklace around Sarah's neck. She reached out and examined it more closely. It was two pieces of stained glass fixed together into a small frame of lead. Inside was a tiny pressed flower.

"Do you like it?" Sarah asked.

"It's lovely. Can I get one?"

Pippa joined Sprog and admired the piece.

Sarah looked directly at Farris.

"It was a present from your father," she said.

Farris looked away.

Nobody said a word for a moment.

"I didn't know whether I'd catch you here," Sarah cleared her throat and continued. "I had to go into Bury for some clay and other things. I just wanted to know when you were likely to be wanting to fire again, so that I could get on."

"I'm sorry," groaned Farris, "it's been hectic, what with the girls and everything."

"Oh that's all right," her eyes twinkled, "I just needed to know, that was all."

Farris led her over to the stained window, crooking his finger for the girls to follow.

"I've been waiting for the okay about this, actually. This is the big one, from the central arch, the one I was telling you about."

They stared at the frame. Each of the square panes around the perimeter showed a scene. Pippa was uncertain of the subject of most of them. There were missing fragments in almost every case. She recognized Lazarus rising from the tomb, but the others were unknown. One figure, dressed in heavy robes, seemed to be peering down an opening in the ground. She thought it might have been a well. One small section of glass was almost painted in miniature—it could not possibly have been seen properly from the church aisles. It reminded

Pippa of an Egyptian painting. A rectangle, shaped like a box, contained an outstretched figure. A line had been drawn from out of the sky, ending at the top of the box. Another figure appeared to be pouring something on top of the figure, suggesting that this might be some kind of bath. The other scenes depicted a gathering of some kind.

The central picture was very badly damaged, and she could already tell where her father had set to work restoring the lead. What remained of the original, showed the upper half of a torso, but the glass ended in a jagged line, at the top of the neck.

The picture continued in the upper right hand section, the hair had been dark. The other fragments suggested that other figures may have been in the original background.

"A portrait, I think," Sarah decided, at length.

"Mmm," agreed Farris, "I think so too, unusual though wouldn't you say? Have you noticed the little insignia disc in the corners of some scenes, almost like a signature?"

Sarah looked closely. A circle, like a seal from a letter, contained a large ornate E.

"Are they all boys and girls?" asked Sprog slowly. She stood close to the window, staring at the figures intently.

"Your daughter's got a good eye for detail," acknowledged Sarah, glancing at Farris.

Sprog's comment made Pippa shudder, she wasn't sure why. She began playing nervously with her fingers.

"Not a lot to go on, but the diocese secretary tells me that there's a good Chauncey Barrow window in Bury Cathedral, so we're going to take a look."

"Ah," exclaimed Sarah, "then you'll need to borrow my mother."

"I'm sorry?" Farris frowned.

"My mother. She's retired, helps me out sometimes,

but she lives in Bury. Knows lots about this area, too. She used to be a guide, I'll get her to meet you."

"Please!" Pippa pleaded, captured by the idea of a proper tour. She stopped pondering over the pendant.

"Can we all come?" asked Bella. Sprog looked up too, interested in anything unusual.

"I don't see why not?"

"Let's say tomorrow at mid-day, we can have lunch too, I'll introduce you. If there's a problem I'll call, but I'm sure there won't be."

"My only problem is a sore hand," Farris flexed his fingers once again, "I suppose a rest tomorrow morning will do me some good."

"Right, that's settled," she said, glancing down at her wrist watch. She gestured that it was getting late and walked briskly to the door. With a turn and a wave she was gone. A light lingered in Farris's face. Pippa nudged Bella's arm.

Sprog ran to the garden window and looked out, hoping she might just see her leave.

Pippa faced the picture in the stained glass again. Her father was still flexing his hand.

"I could help you know?"

"We'll see," he raised an eyebrow and placed the cover back on the top of the frame.

He slapped his hands together in a business like fashion and moved Pippa before him.

"Now, all ears please. I have to take another section out from the church. It's to work on in here, this afternoon. Colour matching. I'm taking Sprog with me, Bella too if she wants, either that or she can stay with you."

"Why, am I staying here?" Pippa asked.

His gaze challenged her to remember.

"What were you going to do? It was your idea and you

never know, it might just help?"

Pippa's jaw fell slack. She had forgotten all about the old records.

"The boxes upstairs. Of course, I was going to have a look through them."

"You still want to don't you?" he frowned.

"Yes . . . yes of course," she couldn't help sounding reluctant. The idea of going back was not very attractive.

"I'll come with you," Bella said sympathetically. "It's daylight too, we'll see much better. It was a silly idea to try and look around up there, the other evening, what with the light being so poor."

"Then that's settled," said Farris. "We won't be long, come on Sprog, come with me. I'm going to chain you up in the church."

Sprog bounced over to the door and opened it.

A turn in the breeze, and the rustle of shifting branches greeted her. She stared at a special corner of the garden for a moment.

SIXTEEN

WHEN THEY reached the church, Farris was surprised to find a pair of workmen in overalls, clambering about on ladders, outside. One was screwing a bracket to the wall, just below the missing window.

Sprog ran ahead and stared up at one of them. His co-worker was struggling to unwind a length of cable, at the top of the other ladder.

"Hallo," said Sprog, boldly.

The workman with the cable looked startled, and then saw Farris approaching in the distance.

"Is that your dad?" he asked.

"He might be."

"Is he the feller' that's working here?"

Sprog nodded, and without waiting for her father or for the workman to continue, she scampered around to the front door of the church and tried the handle. It turned, and within moments she was inside.

Farris watched Sprog disappear into the church. He mildly cursed her impatience, she was a handful. Yet again he wondered if bringing her with him had been such a good idea after all. He looked up at the workmen.

"Mornin'," said the man with the cable. "You the guvnor then?"

"Sort of. You were quick, I only asked for these a day or so ago."

"Tha' Mr Perkins is real efficient, ain't he Sam?"

His partner chuckled.

"Are they thinkin' of opening the place up, then? I s'pose you could sorta floodlight the wood, like a national park."

The partner broke into his private laugh again.

"It's just so that I don't go arse over head if I have to work late," Farris replied. "I may have to do some work here, late in the evening."

"Seems like a lot of trouble to me," muttered the workman, "bet you don't come out here that late. He won't will he, eh Sam?"

This time the pair appeared to share a joke.

Farris became faintly irritated, feeling as though he were the butt of a secret.

"There's electric here we bin' told. Is it on inside?" asked the partner.

"Yeah . . . well, after a fashion," said Farris curtly, surprised they hadn't checked it out for themselves first. "It's the same arrangement as the house, old and basic. The diocese office had a small generator installed as a back-up or to use as an alternative supply."

The workman named Sam sniffed and became serious.

"I'll put a time delay switch in as well, that way you can choose wha' you want. Give you 'nough time to get back to the house safely, or at least out of the grounds here. It's got a long settin' on it, so you'll have plenty of time to get home . . . if you wants."

"Thank you," said Farris turning towards the church door.

"Course," said the partner, "you'll probably be runnin' home so you won't want it too long. Yer don't want to be seein' anything that might care to be followin', eh?"

They both tripped into laughter again. Farris had enough of this and went inside the church.

The musty smell hit head on, as he closed the door behind him. For a moment he thought the place might have changed somehow since he was last here, although there was nothing to suggest this.

The task of restoring the windows suddenly seemed like an impossible feat, although he had worked on larger contracts than St Mary's. The Basilica in Venice had been huge, with more detail per square foot than he had ever encountered before, but he'd got on with it. This job was troublesome, rather than difficult. It also bothered him somehow.

He leaned against a rear pew and stared around the walls. He heard the mumbling of the workmen from outside, but they sounded alien and distant as if the window space was a portal from one time to another.

Farris turned into the aisle and slouched down on to the pew. He scanned the line of other pews ahead of him, dark rows, empty and silent, as though they hosted a congregation of ghosts.

Up ahead, to the left of the central aisle, he saw the top of Sprog's head. Her hair looked unusually ruffled. She seemed to be sitting still, reflecting, just as he was doing. For a moment he thought it strange, Sprog had difficulty in remaining still at the best of times.

Suddenly, he felt a hand against his head.

He lurched forward with a cry of alarm.

"Daddy," whined a voice.

He fell against the pew with a sigh. It was Sprog's hand, and she was standing behind him looking sorry for herself.

"It bit me," she said pitifully.

Farris didn't reply for a second, his throat felt gritty and his stomach fluttered. He reached towards her.

"It's this one," said Sprog, "I was only touching."

Farris examined the hand which Sprog held up for him. There was a red mark across the back, like a weal or a scratch. Sprog stuck her bottom lip out and adopted a hang-dog face.

"How . . . how did you do this?" asked Farris, satisfying himself that it was nothing serious.

Sprog didn't reply, but took hold of her father's sleeve instead, and pulled him out from the pew. He allowed himself to be led across to the far aisle, to a spot beside the scaffolding towers. She pointed towards the wall, wiggling her finger at something within a shadow cast from the scaffolding boards.

He eased himself between the rails and saw a wooden lectern. It would have been at the front usually, some-where beside the organ. He remembered that he had moved it there himself when he was considering making a work space in front of the altar.

"That's just a lectern, Sprog, the Bible is read from it."

Sprog continued to wave her hand and to look upset.

He decided to inspect the thing, to satisfy her.

The stand was oak, and old. Maybe Victorian, he thought. He had been amazed that it was here, and not carted off to some antiques fair.

"Underneath, he bit me from underneath," complained Sprog.

Farris didn't understand what she meant, but looked beneath the book rest. Where the platen met the upright pedestal there was a carved face. He thought it was a bird, eagles were usually found on lecterns. But there was no beak, and despite the baldness of the features, which had suggested a bird to him, the centre was pushed in like a collapsed sack.

Farris turned to Sprog.

"That thing, that bit you?"

Sprog gave a slow, sorrowful nod.

Suddenly one of the workmen called out.

"All right to wire in, guvnor?"

Farris looked towards the empty window, the shuffle of

collapsed aluminium ladders sounded outside.

"Of . . . of course, it's all in the porch I think."

Sprog held out her injured hand.

"Kiss better, Daddy?"

Farris smiled and took Sprog's hand in his. He pushed it to his lips and then pulled her to him in a bigger embrace.

"Are we okay now?"

"Yes!" Sprog turned and gamboled through the gap in the pew.

"Stay close," warned Farris, "I've just got to nip up on to the scaffolding, for a moment."

Taking another glance towards Sprog, to make certain that she was all right, he made his way up the ladder to the scaffolding board.

He reached the top in time to see the end of a ladder disappear around the corner of the building. He poked his head out of the window. Two halogen floodlights had now been fixed below the stone parapet.

Within the church, a chucked bag of tools landed with a clash behind the inner door. He looked down. The workmen were in the lobby. Sprog wandered around the entrance area, next to the sarcophagus. He prayed that she would stay out of trouble, just for a little while longer.

He reached into his apron for his chisel and pliers. The window along from the larger space was cracked and ragged. A corner pane seemed in pristine condition, though. It was a particularly good example of the blue and amber stain which was a feature of most of the glass work in the church. He intended to try and get an exact match for the central window.

He carefully prised the glass away from the H section channel of the lead. Working slowly, he eased the soft lead with the edge of his chisel.

For no good reason, he suddenly looked away from his work down to the pews below. His eye fell on the front row, by the left hand aisle. He stopped working for a moment, grunting at himself for being so edgy, and then resumed.

After a few moments, easing and cajoling, the section came away.

He paused as though something had distracted him.

A flutter, like the wings of a bird, sounded above.

Suddenly, a cold and wet hand slapped the back of his neck.

Farris cried out and staggered back, his fingers clawing at his collar. He wrestled with something leathery, which pulled at his skin. His pulse quickened as he became hot, then he discovered a wet tail.

He grabbed the end and pulled a damp rag away, it wasn't a hand at all.

Pausing for breath, he cast a suspicious look at the tower rail from which it had fallen.

"This is no good," he whispered. "I'm a bundle of sodding nerves."

Again, he found himself peering down at the pew.

Sprog looked up, when she heard her father stumble. He had seemed to recover his footing. She didn't really want to interrupt her new discovery. Crouching at the far end of the sarcophagus, she peered beneath the folds of the altar cloth.

She had found an old friend.

"Another froggy," her voice was filled with delight.

The image was about the size of a small saucer, but was carved in stone relief. It reminded Sprog of the face she had seen on the sundial.

She pulled her head out from the cover and looked over her shoulder, the workmen were making jokes behind the door. It sounded as if they were packing up their things.

Sprog hesitated for a moment, wondering whether she should try the trick or not. Daddy was busy, he wouldn't see her.

"Go on," came a voice. *"Hist whist."*

The same insistent notion she had experienced at the sundial, returned. She felt compelled to act.

With a devilish grin she reached out and held the face, stretching her small hand as widely as she was able, across the surface. The grotesque folds, and deep eye sockets peeked through the gaps in her fingers.

"Maybe," Sprog tried to turn the relief slowly clockwise. For a moment it would not budge, but as with the sundial, something clicked into place to help. There was a rumble from below.

"Oh oh," she sang to herself, and twisted the face quickly in the opposite direction again. Silence fell like a sharply pulled blind.

She dropped the cloth and stood up, as though a naughty child who had been discovered doing something they ought not. She put her hands behind her back and smacked her lips, trying to regain some sense of composed innocence.

The church sounded as hollow and as empty as a robbed tomb.

Up on the scaffolding boards, Farris dropped his pliers and listened. Beyond the stone frame of the vacant window, grey tumbling clouds twisted in on themselves, revealing sudden streaks of veins. They pulled the cloud cover back, revealing rough-edged cracks, as though chunks of the sky were being torn away. A darkness was threatening to break through into day, an unnatural night to blot everything out.

He heard the whistle of the wind, a single haunting note which carried with it a lost voice.

At the same time, a realization hit him like a sudden blow: Sprog had approached from behind to show him her hand.

"That wasn't Sprog," he said slowly. "Who was sitting in the pew?"

He glanced down again, the pews were all empty. Within the church the lobby door opened and a pale, serious-faced workman, looked in, unsmiling this time and saying nothing.

SEVENTEEN

PIPPA STEPPED back and dropped the leather-covered book. Bella felt as though a dark angel had passed by. But there was no sign of any angel, only a vague awareness—a sense of past terrible wrongs.

"Did you feel it?" whispered Bella, swallowing nervously. "Did you?"

The expression on her sister's face gave her the answer.

As Pippa looked through the schoolroom window, she became aware of a far greater sense of evil. In the blink of an eye the day had acquired a burden which was almost as huge as despair.

Pippa could think only of cobwebs; of secret corners and twitching night owls; of dark belfry towers and spectre-haunted graveyards. The play images of a childhood from another time assumed a chilling significance: rocking horses with fierce nostrils, dolls with cross-stitching eyes—vacant and yet knowing, wool pulled from their necks.

The darker side of nursery rhymes suddenly weaved through her thoughts like the twists in a river: of witches in woods and child-eating giants; of strange creatures who could change their appearance at will and deceive. Something of the memory of the place, the room itself, replayed like a recording, instilling a dreadful feeling deep inside her. She heard children's cries, sobbing, and then the voice of one child in particular, again and again.

The coldness slipped through her bones, like quicksilver, easing its way through the marrow. The voice held a message. It was more than simply a cry of personal anguish. It was a warning, unable to express itself clearly.

Suddenly, she felt very frightened indeed as she became aware of a warm trickle weaving down her leg.

EIGHTEEN

THAT EVENING, they ate with an unusual degree of solemnity. A brooding atmosphere had hung about them all day. They had all noticed it. Knowing glances were exchanged between Farris and his two elder daughters. The mood was as plain as a change in the weather, yet it was more complicated than that.

Only Sprog seemed untouched. Her face was ever watchful, like a gleeful sprite, wondering what trick it might get up to next.

At length Farris got up from the table and tried to lighten the moment.

"I've work to do," he announced. "I'm sorry girls, I feel restless. I may turn in later. Remember we have the trip to the Cathedral to see this window. Let's hope the camper van holds out. It was playing up earlier this evening."

Bella began to gather the dishes together.

"I'll do these, Sprog will help this time."

Sprog wrinkled her nose in disapproval. Bella decided to try and be cheery. She looked down at her little sister.

"Then . . ." she began, drawing out the words.

Sprog waited anxiously for the rest of the sentence.

"We can look at the pond, maybe?" she suggested.

"There are big froggies in there," said Sprog, "I've seen them, can we try and catch some?"

"You're disgusting," Pippa declared.

Sprog remained quiet.

PIPPA SAT in an old canvas-covered chair, outside her father's workshop. She had decided to read until bedtime. The evening was still bright, but by bringing a portable

117

spot lead out through the window, she was able to fix a temporary reading lamp.

The note book, that she had discovered earlier in the schoolroom cupboard, lay in her lap. She had found a small collection of papers, too. Some were tightly bound in string, with brown paper around the corner wrappings. Loose leaves were pushed beneath a cardboard sheet in another box, these had escaped being bundled. Pippa took the papers from beneath the notebook and shuffled them into a neat square-edged pack. She angled the spot-light downwards.

A quick perusal suggested snatches of Bible stories, written in different scratchy hands, and in an English which might have been written by older children. This surprised Pippa, thinking only of classes held with slates and a flint scratch crayon or stencil.

One sheet read BEST WORK FOR DR BARROW at the top, and several neat drawings accompanied the writing. Pippa wondered if perhaps this 'Dr Barrow' was strict on presentation? He certainly seemed to like to include sketching.

She leafed through the other pages and found many references to DRAWING TIME. Two brown and crumpled torn sheets looked as though they might have been a timetable. She was puzzled by the hours, they appeared inordinately long and regular, for just a Bible class. She then remembered that Dr Chauncey Barrow had, after all, been an artist. Why shouldn't he have entertained himself by getting the children involved in his own interests?

Pippa tucked the sheets beneath her and opened the book. Instead of beginning to read, she stared across the garden, her gaze holding nothing in particular.

A door slammed inside the house, followed by footsteps and the unmistakable shuffle of Sprog's shoes into gravel. They were going to look at the pond at last.

Pippa returned to her notebook. It was in good condition for its age, bound in a kind of hide, with a small oval brass clip on the side. The pages were crumpled together.

When she opened the front cover, a staleness floated upwards. It was the scent of age. A small insect, resembling a beetle with long horns, scuttled down the side of the first page, disappearing off the edge. It didn't bother her, she'd discovered worse things, scrabbling around old ruins with her mother.

A name was neatly written in faded brown ink, on the inside cover. Pippa shifted the book within the beam of the spotlight to try and make out what it said. It looked something like an abbreviation for Charles—Chas. A surname: Weston, followed. The rest was easy to read—it gave the title: Clerk.

The pages in the front half stuck together firmly. They almost made a single sheet of card. Carefully, she separated the end pages. Taking care not to bend the spine too much, she flattened the book across her knees. Rows of items, almost like a clergyman's shopping list, were spread across the columns. There were orders for altar cloths and cushions in one column, and then appointment times and crosses beside names in another. Most had either Ven. or Rev. beside them.

Pippa examined the next page.

Beneath the heading: Rev. Dr Barrow, was another list, but these were ordinary names, without titles. Most of them were unreadable, the ink having become smudged. Strange sounding surnames were mixed with plainer Christian names. There were Marys and Johns, Smiths, and a Thrumbwad with a Postlethwaite. One, however, was underlined twice: *Sam Stone.*

Pippa paused, and lifted her fingers to her nose. The familiarity of the smell was beginning to irritate her. She wished that she could remember where she had smelt it before.

Two further pages were stuck like glue, but the third came free. The jottings here were scruffily written, as if random thoughts, to remind the writer of things to do. Pippa thought that Mr Weston was particularly fond of lists, and wondered if she wasn't looking at an early example of a filofax.

The next page was arranged into a series of topic headings. The first merely said: *The Grange*; a question mark followed, as though it might have been the subject of further consideration.

The second item featured a now familiar name, again underlined: *Sam Stone*. Beneath this was scrawled: '*to discuss Rev. Dr Barrow's seeming pre-occupation with the child. Much talk amongst the parishioners.*' Lower down she read:

1. General distress in the class.
2. Complaint from mother of Mary Wilson.
3. Letter to be drafted to Ven. Archdeacon.

Beneath this was a note in dark blue ink: '*A grave business. Mrs. Wilson claims Sam Stone made to stand as an artist's model for an 'unpleasant acquaintance of Rev. Barrow' (Mrs. Wilson's description), for an entire day. Dr Barrow claims artist has an illness, a slight skin complaint resulting in a mild discharge, and thus the odour. Modeling was carried out with the child's consent, subject for a new stained glass window*'.

A later note read: '*acquaintance often seen around, co-artist. Employed due to Dr Barrow's condition with his hands, (as discussed with Archdeacon last quarter)*'.

Pippa turned away from her reading and stared across

the garden again. The words were beginning to cloud her mind. Ahead of her, just above the tops of the trees, the gauze moon was faintly visible. Her thoughts turned to Sam Stone and she decided to read no further.

NINETEEN

THE CREATURE crouched in the reeds at the far side of the pond, near the bank. Bella saw it before Sprog did, thinking at first that it might be an otter. It was a dark colour with a skin that glistened. When it moved again, she realized that an otter would have been smaller.

For a moment she thought she saw an eye, it seemed to be watching them.

Sprog was entertaining herself nearby, in front of a cluster of lily pads. She watched the reflection of soft twilight burst into bubbly whorls between the plant life. She was sitting on her haunches, peering and whispering into the water. It was as though the pond and herself were privileged to share an intimate secret, too special to be shared with another, even a sister.

Sprog looked up and saw Bella move her head, from one side to the other, as though trying to ascertain which way round the subject of her attention should be. Sprog jumped up in time to catch the rustle of reeds, where her sister had been looking.

"Ahhh," sighed Sprog, almost in ecstasy. "There you are."

Bella turned sharply on her heels. Sprog's attention was riveted to whatever hid in the reeds.

A whimpering cry accompanied the sound of something being dragged along the ground, almost like an animal with an injured limb. The reeds shuddered again.

Bella watched Sprog's moon-grin.

But then suddenly, for no reason, her face became hard and fierce.

"He's gone now!"

Bella looked back at the reeds, there was only murky blackness between the green lattice work.

"What was it?" asked Bella in a hushed tone.

Sprog's head shot round, the smile returned fully.

"Mister Damp, of course. There's others too, sometimes, but much smaller than him. He's the king froggy. He's got lots of faces. He's clever."

Bella was uncertain how to carry the conversation further.

It was time to go home.

TWENTY

DREAMS RETURNED and filled the night. It brought Pippa books which floated off shelves, books whose pages could not be opened. Images of the stained glass windows at the church, crowded with young faces, rushed before her. Then unexpectedly, a darkness fell and she plummeted, as if drawn downwards into a deep tunnel.

A solitary falsetto voice, clear as ice, sang a madrigal. It soothed, giving a strange peace. A choir of voices joined in from somewhere away in the distance. Soon, the single voice turned to sobs.

It became clear to Pippa whose cry it was. The beautiful boy, with the shivering eyes, was somehow reliving pain.

For a moment the darkness parted and she was back in the schoolroom before the slender figure of the boy. His face was turned away from her. Very slowly, the head turned right round as though it might have been a doll's. The barely open mouth unexpectedly widened.

The smile became unmistakably that of Sprog's.

Pippa sat up with a start as laughter filled her ears.

Only the deep breathing of her sisters', disturbed the stillness. She looked across the room. Light spilled onto the bedroom floor from beneath the door, her father had left a light on, upstairs.

Mouth dry, she crept out of her bed and wrapped a dressing gown around herself. She made her way into the hall, diligently shutting the door after her. She discovered that the light came from her father's room.

Taking care not to wake anybody, she climbed the stairs to the mid-point, and craned her neck to see through the banister rails. She could just about see past the open door. He was sitting, hunched on the edge of the bed. He looked tense as though recovering from another bad dream. His gaze was fixed on the urn, which he held tightly between both hands.

Pippa continued upwards and made soft steps into the bedroom. He looked up with a start, surprised to see her.

"Just a dream," he whispered, between a number of stiffly taken swallows.

"Me too," replied Pippa.

She gently took the urn from his fingers and replaced it on the top of the dresser. He watched her do it, silently. She sat beside him.

"I've been meaning to find a place for that," he sniffed. His eyes looked moist.

"I dreamt about her. I woke up afraid that something was about to happen, something which I couldn't understand. Whatever it was I knew that it was bad. I was drenched with this feeling. I needed something good to pull me out of it, even if it was only a symbol. I held this."

He went silent and then looked directly at her.

"By God, I loved your mother . . ." he broke off as his chin fell down to his chest.

Pippa put her arms around his neck.

"Is it me?" he continued, "I almost cancelled your visit. But I wanted you all to be here so badly."

Pippa hugged him more closely and then pulled her head away. She leveled her eyes with his.

"It's not you. I hear things," she said firmly. "I hear a voice, a cry. It's a boy."

His face registered a flash of alarm, but not surprise. Becoming self-conscious, he licked his lips.

"I don't think it will hurt you, but don't tell the others."

His attempt to lighten the discussion was without

heart. Pippa remained stone faced. He had heard it too, of course he had.

Farris cleared his throat.

"I don't believe in weird occurrences, or whatever you want to call them. I've spent nights in old buildings where I've heard sounds I was unable to account for. Usually it's the wind, there's always some explanation. I've certainly never been harmed by anything strange."

He was finding this conversation difficult.

"Dead is dead, Pippa."

Pippa gave a short laugh.

"Yet you keep mum's ashes?"

He could not help a stare and kissed her on the forehead.

"OK. Maybe there is something here, Bob Ford mentioned a story about a local boy, orphan of course. It had to be. He sang in the choir here. Disappeared one day and was never heard of again. Tales of murder, abduction, you name it. There is a story that it's his voice you hear."

"His name was Sam Stone," Pippa said slowly. "I've been reading a notebook from the schoolroom. I think he was the model for the window you've been working on."

Farris frowned. "Really?"

"Yes, I'll show you the book later, if you like."

"We're going to look at the cathedral and this other window, tomorrow. Sarah's going to meet us there with her mother, remember."

Pippa looked straight into her father's eyes.

"Will you do something for me?" she asked.

Farris's face returned to a relaxed gaze.

"What's that?"

"I want you to have a break one evening soon and take this lady friend out to dinner."

He almost laughed at the suggestion, so grown-up, but

he remembered how late it was and stopped himself. He didn't want to wake the others.

"There's something else," she added. "Will you let me help you do a rough on the window? Just the staining perhaps? You've got behind, and my helping will let you get on with something else. You did promise I could work with you. I think a change would be good too."

He pulled her to him again.

"Yes, all right."

"And," she continued, "Mum's ashes are to go into a proper resting place when you finish here?"

He felt as though he was receiving advice from a wise and experienced counselor. She had grown with a maturity which almost frightened him.

"It's a deal."

They heard the creak of a door behind them. Pippa turned round. Her sisters stood in the doorway. Sprog looked concerned and Bella stared with sleepy eyes.

"Daddy," said Sprog, "what's the matter?"

"Nothing," Farris replied firmly, "nothing at all."

Sprog ran over to him and climbed on his lap. Bella followed. All three 'Imps' were now together, and they stayed there with him until dawn crept slowly through the window.

TWENTY ONE

As Farris drove through the village, it suddenly occurred to Pippa that this was the first time that they had left the Grange, since their arrival. Her father had talked of 'going into the village' on several occasions. Only now did it strike her, that he had made no effort to show them the place, or let them meet any locals other than Bob Ford.

Bob Ford kept well out of their way now. Pippa knew that it was something to do with the work that her father was doing at the church. It seemed to make sense. He had clearly been commissioned to carry out a job that certain locals didn't want doing.

The engine labored; Farris cursed some mysterious mechanical part, more than once. Sprog was quiet, but Bella was her usual neutral and correct self, sitting quietly. Only Pippa noticed people's faces as they passed by neat rows of thatched roofs and tiny pan-tiled buildings, set back from the road. Some people pointed, whilst others made cursory nods. A sudden smile would occasionally break through a mask face: plastic and insincere.

"It's not a very big place, is it?" decided Pippa, half expecting to have seen more houses.

Her father was flexing his fingers as he steered, his hand felt better this morning.

"Nope," he replied. "They're friendly, but they keep themselves to themselves. I've given up somewhat, haven't the time to worry about public relations on a brief visiting contract, it is just business after all."

Pippa recalled the odd attitude of the workmen, when they fixed the halogen lamps. She decided that perhaps her father was right to keep a certain distance. She decided not to press him further.

The line of cottages stopped abruptly and after a corner, the road took a dip. Sweeping open countryside showed a bare grey day. The weather had turned cooler and on the horizon, rain threatened. In the distance lay miles of fields, parted by the gentle sweep and incline of the road. Pippa settled down to enjoy the ride, and the unusual broody quiet of the 'Sproglodyte'.

After a while, in the distance, empty fields were replaced with terraced blocks and parked cars. As they approached the town centre, Pippa noticed the signs of recently-arrived industrial life, with garages and estate complexes.

"Soon be there," chirped Farris, suddenly cheering up.

Bella nudged Pippa with her elbow and winked.

FARRIS PARKED the camper van at the rear of a super-market, a walk away from the cathedral. This gave the girls the opportunity to sample a flavour of the city. They nosed in shop windows whilst ambling casually along the High Street and, eventually, into the side turnings.

Farris explained that almost anywhere in the city was never very far from the cathedral. The tower loomed over the streets like a look-out post.

They chatted as they walked more briskly, their shoes crisply echoing in narrow 'pedestrian only' turnings. Pippa tried to piece together scraps of church history for Bella, giving her the odd fact or two whilst Farris ploughed ahead. He worried, in case they might be late. Sprog was still in her own world. She made side-long looks down streets, as if expecting to see someone she knew.

At the bottom of a semi-cobbled lane, they turned a corner and arrived at the front of the cathedral.

Sarah Prestwood and her mother were waiting, as arranged, in front of the west face. They stood across from a well cared patch of grass, dwarfed by the grey stone entrance that grew behind them. Sarah Prestwood hesitated when she saw them, but confident that it was the Farris family, gestured furiously. The tightly knit band broke into quick walks and runs.

Sprog ran to Sarah and hung on to her hand with unashamed familiarity. Sprog noticed that she was wearing the stained glass necklace again. The amber glass caught a glint of struggling sunlight, as the pendant bounced against her sweater.

"Hi!" called Farris as he crossed into the shelter of the building. He nodded at the short, plump woman, who stood beside Sarah. She wore jeans and a sweater which appeared to match her daughter's. A pair of spectacles hung around her neck from a chain.

Sarah introduced her mother as Mrs Prestwood. They took turns in shaking hands, in a somewhat formal fashion. Pippa noticed that her father shot a particular smile at Sarah.

"You can take the 'tour' in whatever form you'd like," said Sarah. "Mum knows the window you want to see. She knows a fair deal about the Grange and St Mary's as well. She thinks you'll be disappointed with the example here though, I'm afraid."

"Excuse me," Mrs Prestwood glared at her daughter. "I do have a voice."

Sarah Prestwood pursed her lips.

"It's small and a bit of a hotch potch," continued Mrs Prestwood, "the work of more than one person. Then again, you think you may have the answer to all that. If you'd like, I'll take the girls round the whole caboodle after, you can join us or we can have tea inside and all meet up for lunch? Whatever?"

Farris agreed, a ready-made programme was not to be passed over.

"That sounds fine. Let's see how we go. It's good of you to spare the time."

"No problem, my dears," said Mrs Prestwood, "I love the place. Full of relics, illuminated history. Did the tours professionally till recently, then had to retire. My legs you know."

There was a touch of something warm, almost folksy about her voice.

"Shall we do it, then?" Sarah asked, making a wide gesture with her arms for them to enter the cathedral. Sprog gave her usual big grin as they proceeded up the steps, and into the shadows.

Bella caught Sprog making a small and secretive acknowledgement to someone.

As soon as they entered the building, Mrs Prestwood started up her commentary. She adopted a single steady tone, turning herself one way and then the other, her head tilted upwards slightly. Her hands gesticulated busily, as though rehearsing a well worn piece of rhetoric.

Sarah resisted a laugh as Mrs Prestwood's cheeks filled with an apple colour. Farris watched in amazement, the girls were in awe. Pippa listened politely. Bella and Sprog just staggered like penguins. They stared up at the lofty heights of the arcades, with arms outstretched to steady themselves.

There were very few people in the cathedral. The ring of their voices echoed along with the thin tinkle of footsteps.

"Hang on a minute, Mum," Sarah insisted, pulling at her mother's sleeve.

Mrs Prestwood was interrupted in mid flow, reciting a

speech about the place having 'once been a Monastic community, almost 1300 years ago'.

Mrs Prestwood's hand hovered in the air, her mouth half open.

"Just a few bits and pieces with the girls, but Kit really wants to have a look at the window from St Mary's."

Mrs Prestwood gave a solid stare and gestured to them to follow her.

She walked slowly, leading them down the northern arcade aisle. Murky light lit the ceilings, making the place a sombre, yet stunning, mixture of complex stone shapes.

"It's in a little Chapel, just along here, tucked into a corner. With the shortage of examples of stained glass, I've never fully understood why it's been left in such a gloomy spot. But I suppose . . ." she trailed off as though she had suddenly thought of an answer to her question.

She stopped unexpectedly, beside a window that was tucked into a side arch. She put her finger to her lip, deep in thought, and then signaled to Farris to move closer.

"Ah, I forgot these, as you're working on St Mary's?"

She pointed towards the ceiling of the transept, in a far corner, where the wall met the roof, were rows of wall paintings. Only one of these was easily identifiable as a group of figures, orange light from a circular domed window lit the scene. It was in poor condition, but strong blues and ambers hinted at a distinct style.

Farris stared at it for longer than Mrs Prestwood expected, as if he had seen something of particular importance.

"Twelfth century," she announced, interrupting his silence with the tour guide voice again. "Thought it might be of interest, considering. Painted by the monk artist known as Edric, although we now believe that may not have been his real name."

Pippa sucked her breath in recognition.

Farris murmured, then realized that he had not fully understood her.

"Of interest, considering?" he repeated.

He looked back at the design again. There was something about it, something familiar that nagged at the back of his mind, an aspect of the style perhaps, was it the colours?

"There's a postcard of this, at the souvenir shop, I think," continued Mrs Prestwood. "You can get a good look at it then."

"Good . . . good," Farris continued to stare upwards. "Why did you say— 'considering'?"

The formality dropped from her voice suddenly.

"Well he isn't in there any more of course, the church I mean. Surely you knew that Edric was buried in the stone tomb, at St Mary's? Only briefly, though."

Pippa turned her head towards her father.

"That diocese man rang and told me, I've not explained it all to you yet." Pippa turned back to Mrs Prestwood. "You mean the sarcophagus—the tomb at the head of the aisle?"

"Why, yes, that's where it is, I think," said Mrs Prestwood with a sniff. "Bad chap by all accounts, our Edric. Do you like stories?"

"Everyone likes stories!"

"Well, then. The tomb is without a name, you must have noticed that? Edric worked in the church, you see, this was before they named it St Mary's, the entire quarter was the site of a Monastery. Edric was an illustrator."

"We thought . . ." began Farris.

"Yes, yes," said Pippa hurriedly, interrupting her father. "We knew some of that. Do you know why he was a 'bad chap' though?"

Mrs Prestwood went into 'tour-guide mode', again.

"It's only folk tale of course, but he is said to have indulged in heathen practices and ceremonies. This is according to some late letters, Monastery records. He was excommunicated, eventually. He consorted with devils, made sacrilegious deals in return for his powers. Some said he could cast the glamour over people, you know— charm them, put them under a spell. Make them see what he wanted them to see. It's said he could fly at night and could change his form, Shape-shift they used to call it."

"Shape-shift?" Farris narrowed his eyes.

"Most fairies, wizards and witches can do it, so goes fairy-lore. Sometimes the Shape-shifter is known as a Hoodie, too. You must have heard of Shape-shifting. Have you never heard the folk song The Two Magicians? Sometimes it's called The Coal Black Smith? Our Sarah knows it, don't you? Go on Sarah."

Sarah Prestwood began to sing, very softly:

"He looked out the window as black as any soot,
She looked out the window as white as any milk,
Hallo hallo hallo hallo, you coal black smith,
A maiden I shall die,
(I'm not sure of the next bit),
I'd rather die a maid than be buried all in my grave,
You never shall have my maiden-head,
That I have kept so long . . ."

She stopped singing and looked a little embarrassed.

"I think I've got some lines mixed up. It goes on— about how they transform themselves into various crea- tures, he in pursuit of her, each time changing shape to elude capture."

"Then there's the last verse," said Mrs Prestwood.

"Well, yes but . . ."

Sarah looked uncomfortable and stared at her feet.

"Well go on, scary stuff, isn't it?"

Sarah shook her head.

Mrs Prestwood recited, rather than sang. "She became a corpse, a corpse all in the ground, and he became the cold clay and smothered her all around. . . ."

She was unsmiling, and decided to recite no further. The last few words of her verse sounded hollow in the vastness of the building.

Farris shivered, not certain that the chill of the Cathedral was the reason for his unease or something about learning that Shape-shifters were also known as the Hoodie. He recalled Sprog's words about her imaginary friend, something about a hood. There was no logic in the connection, it just disturbed him.

"The Two Magicians?" whispered Pippa.

"That was what this monk became, I suppose," Mrs Prestwood continued, "a magician. A magician artist. He bewitched his paints, too. It is said that he could capture his subject's souls in one of his drawings or paintings. He is supposed to have illustrated many books of hours and calendars but they were all burnt. Nothing survives, except a few pages in a collection here—just drawings of animals not people. He drew from life you see."

Pippa started to fidget, moving her weight from one foot to the other.

"He had no shortage of folk wanting to have their picture drawn. That was, of course, before they found out about his black talent. When he completed the drawing he took a part of them with it, caught it there in the picture. He even had an official accuser, another monk whom he used as some kind of model for one of his illuminated manuscripts. The accuser said that his eternal soul was in peril, that this Edric owned it. The abbot was supposed to have sought advice from very high up."

She raised her face towards the ceiling, suggesting divine consultation.

"I know that all his work was ripped out of the church," said Pippa, "but what about this?"

"Moonlighting," said Mrs Prestwood, smiling.

Pippa did not understand.

"One of the earliest examples I'd say," chirped Farris, faintly amused by the idea, "work on the side, Pippa. So they missed this one."

"They let it stay, there was an enormous row about it. I'll show you something interesting: look at it again."

The little group turned and stared at the paintings. This corner of the church had emptied.

"Do you see the white shape, like the outline of a bird, in the centre of that end figure? There's one in another figure too, but you can't see it easily now, flaking paint and age."

They stared intently. It was difficult to tell with any certainty what the pictures were supposed to show. But there was something odd: a pale coloured outline in a central area of one panel.

"It's only just like a bird," Farris remarked.

"A dove, Mr Farris. It was painted into the picture afterwards by the abbot himself. The story goes that they did it with a special service, it was almost an exorcism if you like. He decreed that it should be carried out to safeguard the souls of those whose image had been used in the picture. You see, a soul in peril could be saved if some token of goodness, of a pure love, was added to the drawing of the victim. It was no use just destroying the thing. I believe a dove and a cross was drawn into the page of a manuscript for the accuser monk. To be honest, they tried to hush it up, about these pictures I mean." Then she added with a wry smile, "Don't know if the symbols worked, of course. But symbols can be very powerful. Very powerful indeed."

"The accuser was Master Hugo," said Pippa softly, remembering her conversation with Mr Perkins.

"I think you're right," Mrs Prestwood admitted. She was taken aback by Pippa's occasional scene stealing.

Mrs Prestwood lowered her voice.

"Edric died suddenly, there was no explanation, except that he was found in quite a state. He was all puffed up and almost black, with heavy folds of loose skin. His evil had got the better of him in some way. The abbot proclaimed that it was God who struck him down, whilst he was changing form, Lord knows from what. He went out at night you see, as an animal they said. Many village folk told stories of waking late with something heaving beneath the bed clothes. A rat or stoat or whatever, but they said it was him. Eventually, the whole business got out of hand. Was said that children had gone missing, gone mad. It sounded a dreadful affair. Later, when all the gossip about it went round, the monk's order decided to get rid him for good. It wasn't a fitting tale for Holy Men. His body was taken from the tomb, very soon after they'd laid him there. Supposed to have been put somewhere else. Somewhere else for good."

Her last words hung on the stillness.

Mrs Prestwood caught the seriousness of the expressions that circled her.

"It's only a story, my loves. I know more about it than most though. You see, I was going to write a long article on the subject for a glossy magazine in London. I spent a whole year on researching, and I learned a bit of Latin too. They didn't want it in the end. Said it was piffle." She stood stiffly to attention and sighed. "I suppose it is all stuff and nonsense, really. I'm sure the story's been exaggerated over the years, and a lot has been forgotten of course. Dr Barrow stole the show somewhat, you see. He was an odd one too by all accounts."

"Wasn't he given his marching orders as well?" Pippa asked.

Mrs Prestwood looked surprised.

"Yes, he was actually. You're not from these parts, are you? How do you know?"

"Let me guess?" said Pippa. "He frightened the local children, by wanting to draw them for his windows. There was a complaint about a boy named Sam Stone wasn't there?"

"Yes," Mrs Prestwood replied, "I do believe his name was something like that. Had a thing about him, what would you call it exactly? An obsession about his beauty? I don't think it was anything more than that. How did you know all this?"

"I found a notebook upstairs at the Grange, although most of the pages were difficult to read. There was enough there to give me an idea of what it was all about. It's funny how Edric and Rev Barrow were both artists."

Mrs Prestwood appeared to consider this for a moment. Was Pippa suggesting something? Feeling that she might have a sympathetic listener to folklore, she suddenly leaned forward and whispered.

"Have you seen the ghost?"

Bella flinched. Pippa and Farris exchanged looks. Sarah Prestwood had stood quietly by, fascinated by all she was hearing. Her lips parted in surprise. It was obvious that much of this was news to her.

Farris butted in.

"We . . . we have heard that there was one once." Then he quickly added: "We've not seen anything though."

He made to look at his watch.

"I am sorry," said Mrs Prestwood, standing to attention and taking the hint. "Come on, I'll show you the Barrow window."

She led the way down the aisle arcade to a small side chapel. The space was ill-lit, like a cavern. Here she pointed to a small corner window.

Farris and Pippa hurried over to it.

The window was intact, but a bad example of Victorian glass. The central panel showed a crowd of young faces, one face appearing to have been added later, and in a different style. It was a bit of a mess. Pippa stared at it for a long time, she had seen something like it, somewhere before.

"Our Dr Barrow, but plus assistant I would say," Farris declared after only a moment's thought.

"The assistant? Do you mean the apprentice?" asked Mrs Prestwood with an interested smile.

"Yes," said Farris curtly. "But I'm not so sure anymore who was the apprentice and who was the master."

"Don't mean to bang on as though we've got loads of oddities out here, but he was reckoned to have been peculiar. Kept out of sight they say, wore this big cloak. I believe he disappeared when Dr Barrow left, perhaps they left together?"

"What was wrong with Dr Barrow?" asked Pippa.

"Just a problem with his hands, some disease," said Mrs Prestwood, "that's why he got his friend in to help. It was a very strange business. People don't like the quarter, the church, rectory or the land. No wonder too. It's always had trouble. I was very surprised when my daughter told me that you were working there. Local folk don't like it at all and they'll clam up if you try and ask them anything. I suppose this new diocese secretary is responsible."

"Young Mr Perkins?" Farris asked.

Mrs Prestwood smiled. She had obviously met him.

Pippa turned to the figures in the window again.

The additional face was from her dreams, but there was something else that struck home, something that particularly bothered her.

"It's . . . it's a boy," she murmured to herself, "but . . ."

Pippa kept the rest of her thoughts unspoken. Particularly because the face could have easily passed as an image of Sprog. Behind her, the early afternoon shadows lengthened across the floor of the cathedral. She felt nervous and apprehensive again.

She looked about for Sprog, but she was nowhere in sight. With a huge sigh, Pippa realized that she had slipped away somewhere.

TWENTY TWO

BELLA THOUGHT that she had seen Sprog only a moment earlier, or at least someone just like her, back in the main arcade. But she decided that it wasn't her sister when the little girl began holding hands with an old woman, bent double in a huge black dress. The pair seemed to know one another and Sprog obviously didn't know anyone here.

Farris became alarmed, desperately scanning the spaces around him for any sign of his daughter. The spaces were framed by pillars and piers, as though each in itself was a window scene.

Sarah reached out and held his arm reassuringly.

"She'll be here somewhere. Come on, Mum knows the layout inside out."

"You don't know her, though," Farris returned. "She climbs into things, explores, gets herself lost."

Pippa ran ahead into the central aisle, with Bella in pursuit.

"She can't be in any danger, Mr Farris." Mrs Prestwood tried desperately to sound hopeful, "not here. This is a holy place."

Farris shot her a look that told her that he was unconvinced.

"So is the church."

"Let's split up and meet by the souvenir shop, down by the entrance," suggested Sarah. "Say, in ten minutes?"

The group dispersed, Farris went ahead and caught up with Pippa. She had begun to look over a small side chapel, along from the transept.

Methodically, she worked her way along a row of

oak pews.

"Back at the souvenir shop in ten minutes, okay?" repeated Farris, "I'm going to look outside."

Pippa nodded, but as she did so, her attention was suddenly drawn to something behind her father.

"Look!"

He turned on his heels.

Walking towards them, hand in hand with Bella, was Sprog, with her head bowed low.

Farris ran towards Sprog, almost tripping himself up. His hand shook as his outstretched finger pointed towards her with a warning.

Sprog began to bubble up with tears even before her father had said anything. Behind her, came Sarah and her mother, their faces displaying obvious relief.

"I told you. She wouldn't have gone far," Mrs Prestwood said with a smug face. "Let's all go and get some late lunch after Mr Farris has got his postcard of the wall painting."

Farris suddenly felt sorry that he had shouted at Sprog. He crouched down and lifted her chin. She wiped her hand across her cheek. A wet green mark remained there.

Farris thought, *I knew it, bloody ponds, again*, but decided to say nothing. Instead he wiped the mark away with a handkerchief, instantly provided by Pippa.

"You went outside, didn't you?" he asked.

Sprog mumbled a quiet, "No."

Sarah crouched down beside him and pulled a face at Sprog, managing to engage a glimmer of a returning smile.

Sprog reached out and held Sarah's glass pendant, whilst sniffing back further tears.

Pippa joined them. She took the pendant from Sprog and looked at it closely. The pressed flower between the glass, made a mysterious shape. It was well done. Then she had an idea.

"Sproglodyte. I'm going to get you one of these. I'm going to make it myself."

Pippa looked back at her father, as if seeking his permission. His warm eyes gave approval.

"It's going to be very special though," she added. "Very special indeed."

Sprog beamed with joy.

AFTER A light lunch, the rest of their day in Bury was pleasantly spent, walking around the market, looking in shops and drinking afternoon tea.

Pippa kept dropping hints in front of Sarah Prestwood about how her father might like a night out sometime soon; how he needed a break somewhere, and so on. Farris glared at Pippa so regularly that his eyes almost became permanently wide and red. Sarah pretended not to understand. She was flattered by Pippa's efforts.

The journey back to the Grange was noisier than the ride there, even though the passengers hardly spoke a word. Pippa thought that the engine was in danger of rattling itself loose. Farris gritted his teeth and assured them that he knew what was wrong, and that it was not as serious as it sounded.

Eventually, the road turned into the village and they took the dirt road off towards the house. They passed in front of the pond, but this evening, even in the early light, the place looked drab. There was none of the ambiguous, strange beauty that they encountered when they first arrived. It was now simply little more than 'an old house'. Pippa wondered if it might be the weather that reinforced the effect. She decided to put it out of her mind when other, stranger notions, suddenly began to occur to her.

*   *   *

WHILST SPROG sat quietly at the table, Pippa hurried upstairs as soon as her father went across to the church. Shortly afterwards she locked herself away in the studio, leaving strict instructions that nobody was to enter the room.

Farris had wanted to check on the halogen floods, but he had also taken with him the last dog-eared post-card of the monk's painting, which he had bought at the souvenir shop.

He sat in the church alone, ignoring the crawl of the damp air and the rising mustiness, which smelled like stale dough. For a long while he kept gazing alternately at the postcard, and then up at the stained glass windows. The light around him was beginning to play tricks, corners appeared to shift with twists of shadow.

He had wondered if it was his fancy, or whether it was possible that there was a link between the monk's painting and the stained glass in the church. Something of the style was similar—the colours in particular. That was what had bothered him at the cathedral. He reasoned that Barrow and his assistant might have been influenced by the work in the cathedral, they would almost certainly have seen it there after all, but now he was mystified by the occasional circled E, found on some of the Victorian examples. It made him wonder.

Dr Barrow's assistant could have been called Edmund or Eric, he supposed.

Eventually, with a sigh, he rose and decided that he was imagining things. There were centuries between the artists, it would take a real expert to give a proper opinion.

He made a resolution to pull himself out of the mood. Tomorrow he would allow Pippa to get started on the

window, and he decided to make a date with Sarah
Prestwood.

TWENTY THREE

SPROG SEEMED oddly tired the next morning, and was more irritable than usual. She had to be scrubbed hard by Bella: spots of green stain stubbornly remaining on her fingers. When Bella had finished, a peculiar black mark remained on Sprog's skin, like a bruise.

When she finally arrived at the table, she noticed an unusual silence from the rest of the family. It was not, however, a gloomy silence. An undercurrent of fun and expectation threatened to burst through at any moment.

As she climbed up on to the stool she saw that a little bundle of coloured tissue paper had been put beside her plate. She had been left a present. Carefully she unwrapped the tissue and gasped as a cord fell from the paper. On closer inspection, she realized that there were tiny beads threaded onto a string. It was something else, which lay beneath this, that made her practically purr with pleasure: it was a stained glass pendant.

"Go on," said Farris, "Pippa made it for you, specially."

"And you designed it, remember?" added Pippa. "Remember the drawing you did?"

Sprog lifted the necklace carefully. A heart shape of yellow glass was sandwiched by a border of lead. It was like the one which her father had made for Sarah, only Sprog decided that this one was better.

Her eager fingers unraveled the cord, and then, very slowly and carefully, she put it around her neck.

"Say thank you," Farris prompted.

Pippa leaned over and kissed Sprog on the forehead. The pendant bounced loosely against the front of her T-shirt. Sprog picked up the heart shape and examined it closely. Instead of a pressed flower, it was filled with tiny granules, like sand.

"Thankyou, Pippa," she said, almost over politely.

Farris raised an eyebrow.

"Nice work there."

"The cord is a bit long," decided Bella. She rose to adjust it to a smaller fit.

"I'll make you a proper cord, or we can get you a chain," said Farris.

Sprog glowed.

FARRIS DECLARED the day to be 'a day of catching up on work'. He had risen early, expecting that Bob Ford might be calling. A moment of annoyance surfaced when there had been no sign of the man. It was as though he had abandoned them.

There had been rain during the night, although neither Bella or Sprog remembered the sounds of any pitter patter on the windows or roof. Pippa thought she had heard wind and the rustling of leaves against the back door in the early hours, but that was all.

Bella ventured out and sniffed the air. She reported that it was too damp to go out yet. She suggested that Sprog and she might play together upstairs, in the school-room.

Although there had been no agreement made between them, Farris and Pippa said nothing more about the sounds that they heard, or thought they heard. Pippa searched out her father's face when Bella mentioned the schoolroom. He gestured with a tilt of his head to let the subject pass.

Then it was down to work.

Father and daughter worked through the morning, without a break. Farris had previously made sketches of several faces, which he thought were in keeping with the style of the existing church windows. He purposely involved Pippa with the decision over which head should be fixed on to the ragged edged neck. They could not decide if the original had been the work of Barrow or the mysterious apprentice, although Pippa was now firmly convinced that it was originally a portrait of Sam Stone.

Pippa chose the sketch which least looked like the face she had seen in her dreams. It was a plain drawing with little detail, a young person's face, which could have belonged to anybody.

Farris wondered whether to bother with a dummy window. Time had become precious, but he decided to gauge the effect within the church, before embarking on anything further. Pippa was helping him this time too, and that would speed things.

They divided the task. He concentrated on painting the outline onto a sheet of plain glass, set above the chosen sketch. Meanwhile, Pippa opened the lead in the old window with the lathekin—the special chisel that he used to widen out the flat outside lead. This allowed the glass to fit into the section easily.

Farris explained that he was going to leave the border panels for the time being, still perplexed by what some of them were meant to represent. He had compiled a list of possibilities from the remains of the damaged frames, but he decided that he would create his own if necessary, even if it meant inventing scenes.

Towards lunchtime, Sprog and Bella joined them. Sprog stood silently in the doorway and looked across the room, to where the empty window waited for the dummy insert. The ragged edges were straightened up with new lead sections. Bella squeezed past Sprog and went over for a better view. The lead had been opened cleanly and neatly. Bella inspected the job, whilst Pippa stood puffed with pride at her handiwork.

"Don't you think she's done well?" said Farris. He was delighted, secretly.

"It looks odd, a neck without a face," Bella remarked.

"I've finished the face," he replied, "the glass is over there on the work board waiting to dry, and then we add the staining."

Sprog remained in the doorway. She looked in on the scene without emotion or interest.

"Come on, Sprog," said Farris. "Take a look at the face."

Almost reluctantly, she stepped into the room and crossed to where they were working.

She craned her neck to see over the edge of the work board. Neutral eyes surveyed the outline. Her pendant rubbed against the edge of the table.

"What do you think?" asked Farris.

Sprog murmured something and went to look out of the window.

"The weather looks all right now," she said, without turning away from the pane.

Pippa shrugged her shoulders as her father sighed between his teeth.

"She's in a funny mood," he whispered, nodding in Sprog's direction. "Never mind, let's get a bite, even if madam has the hump."

He squeezed Pippa's arm.

"You've done well. In fact my confidence in you has risen. It's a little while since we worked together, I'd forgotten how good you were."

Pippa pretended to shine her nails on her bib, and re-arranged her hair back from her face. He was genuinely impressed, and although he had played it down, he had been more than a little surprised at the quality of the heart pendant. The sand had been a novel idea too.

"Sarah's dropping by to return some bits and pieces later," he continued, as he wiped his hands on a rag. "If we get back to it shortly, we can get this out of the way. She might take it with her for firing if the kiln is free, and then tomorrow we could set it in the stone frame. I'm going to fix a support for it in the church."

"What about staining?" asked Pippa.

Farris held her squarely in front of him.

"That, I shall leave entirely to you! Show Bella and Sprog how to do it. We'll have a family business going yet. I've decided, no expense spared."

She shone, that was far more than she expected.

Bella rubbed her hands together with excitement at the prospect. In the meanwhile, Sprog watched intently through the garden window.

LATER THAT afternoon, Sarah Prestwood called and collected the glass. Farris made much of Pippa's achievement, enthusing proudly in front of Sarah. The colours were perfect, with a harmony that complemented the others. He was eager to see the window in place, in the church.

Pippa helped Sarah put the glass in the rear of her estate car, fastidiously arranging blankets around it as though it was a new born child. Bella and Sprog watching quietly.

"I don't think you trust me with it," said Sarah.

"Of course I do, it's just that . . ."

"I know," she replied, "I'm only leg pulling. Why not come with me and watch the firing?"

"There's not exactly a lot to see," Farris chipped in, "but if Pippa wants . . ."

"I'd love to," said Pippa, as she turned towards her

father. "Can I?"

Farris opened his arms with a shrug.

"Could I stop you?"

TWENTY FOUR

SARAH PRESTWOOD'S estate car sped along winding country roads. Pippa found the car quieter and smoother than the old camper van, and for the first time felt oddly warm and secure.

As they made their way, the trees on the horizon bowed with slow, steady gestures. The night was falling fast now, there was none of the orange light which Pippa had admired during the earlier evenings of her arrival. The sky had been cloudy all day, with brief spells of drizzly rain. Worse weather now threatened.

Suddenly, they passed through a cavern of greenery that opened out to an unexpected bend. Here, typical Suffolk cottages of pan-tile and timber-frame ran along one side of the road, whilst more open fields stretched away on the other.

They had arrived. The journey had not taken long.

Sarah's cottage stood apart from a block of terraced houses, up on an embankment. It was a long flint rubble building, with red pan tile roofing that made a series of ragged edges. This gave the house a run-down appearance, although, as Pippa later learnt, the inside was immaculate, if a little untidy. They drove past the house and up on to an unmade drive.

They had spoken little in the car. It was Pippa who finally broke the silence as they pulled into the front of a walnut-stained ship-lap workshop.

"That's your studio, then?" she asked, as an automatic light lit the frontage.

"Certainly is," came the reply, grateful for the question. "I thought we might get this straight into the kiln if that's okay."

"Is it just the same as firing pots?" asked Pippa as they reversed into the car port.

"No. No it's not. Your dad came here and did his own to begin with, but . . ." she started to laugh, "well, he insisted on teaching me, and I was willing, I must admit. I overfired some trial stuff at first but I've got it right now."

"This is only a try-out as well, so I don't think it will matter that much."

"Wait and see," said Sarah as if she might know different. "He's impressed with what you've done, really he is. Restoration is an expensive business, from the point of view of both time, and materials. Do you really think he'd let you continue with the project if he wasn't considering actually using your work?"

Pippa went quiet, allowing Sarah's words to sink in. Was it possible that her father might use her work in the actual window?

It had started to rain again, so they hurried from the car. Sarah rushed to the front of the workshop and wrestled with a bunch of keys, whilst Pippa opened the Volvo's rear door. After a moment Sarah returned, and together they carried the glass into the workshop.

The place was single storey, but the roof was lofty with a series of stained tie beams, which crossed the width of the room. Pottery mobiles, and similar examples hung from them. There were two long benches that ran down the centre. Other tables, along the sides, were crowded with pots and pedestals. It reminded Pippa of her father's own workshop, except that there were no sheets of glass to be seen and the smells were different. The atmosphere here was warmer, cosier than the Grange. She felt more relaxed and resisted the urge to constantly glance into corners and to look over her shoulder.

Two kilns stood at the far end of the room, like a pair of ugly squat grey boilers.

"Come on," said Sarah. "We'll 'closed fire' it at 450 degrees, and let it cool overnight, that should do the trick. The kiln's been on during the day so it'll not take long to heat up. There's a timer too, so we've no need to baby-sit. Tomorrow morning we'll whip it back to your dad. He was right really, there isn't much to see, but I'm glad of the company."

They moved the glass sheet to a small table beside the right hand kiln. The kiln now seemed to be watching them with a single red light eye.

"Luckily there's no lead work in this window panel, Pippa muttered, "handling it afterwards can be tricky. I mean to get it into place up into the stone. It flexes, see?"

Sarah switched the temperature bell on and slapped her hands together.

"Are you going to be a stained glass artist?"

"Probably. It's the history I like more than anything. Oldness is fun, if you know what I mean. Dad's always involved us with his work, and sometimes I got to see him a lot if he was working here in England."

Sarah leaned against the wall.

"He had a big contract in Venice didn't he?" she asked, raising her eyebrow.

"Yes, at a church in St Mark's Square. He works everywhere. Aunt Emma says that it's so that he can make enough quick money to get us together again."

Sarah detected a note of uncertainty in her voice.

"You don't sound completely convinced," she said quietly.

Pippa heaved her shoulders.

"Mum's death hit him terribly. It wasn't expected. They'd been students together and all that. I think something happened to him and he just wanted to get away for a while, even from us—though he loved us. We stayed with his sister and then Bella and me went to this school. Sprog's there with us now."

She paused before continuing, snatching a moment's thought.

"I'm not saying that the 'quick earning to make a better future' isn't true, I just think it was a convenient idea. I remember he used to look at me in a funny way. I think I reminded him of mum too much. That was the real problem. I'm not sure if I should be flattered or not. Anyway, we're going to see more of him now."

"I think your dad might have felt just a little bit guilty about all that."

Pippa looked up, surprised by the remark. Her father must have been sharing some very personal thoughts with her. Sarah Prestwood immediately wished she had bitten her tongue and turned to check the kiln.

In a matter of minutes the bell rang. The correct temperature had been reached and they lifted the glass into the kiln.

After she shut the door, Sarah Prestwood stood quietly, her arms hung by her sides as if she no longer knew what to do with them. She felt somehow intimidated by Pippa, it was just something to do with the strength of the girl's character. She hesitated before she spoke.

"Are you much like your mother?" she asked directly.

Pippa stared at her. For a fleeting moment she was not sure what was meant by the question. She stiffened, holding her shoulders straighter than usual.

"Some think so. Dad does. I suppose I look a bit like her. We got on as friends you see—not just mother and daughter." She cast her gaze down to the floor, and then looked up again. "Do you like Dad?"

Sarah's face became serious. Her eyes shuddered gently.

"Yes," she replied, barely hearing the breath in her reply, and surprised by the speed of her response.

The kiln buzzed and they heard a click from somewhere at the rear of the motor, a noise like a thermostat. It broke the tension of the moment perfectly.

"Come into the house," said Sarah, using the interruption to change the subject. "I'll show you the bedroom. Then we'll have something hot, and maybe we can chat?"

Pippa relaxed into an easy amble and led the way to the front of the workshop. As they closed the door behind them, and just as Sarah switched out the light, Pippa thought she heard a muffled noise, like a voice, maybe a small cry. It was nothing recognizable, but for a second it caused her to look back. She decided it must have been the heat.

The noise had come from inside the kiln.

DESPITE THE friendly atmosphere of the cottage, Pippa had strange dreams again, that night. She dreamt that she was somewhere black and cold, and it was wet too—a slimy wetness that she felt whenever she reached out her hand. Smells that belonged in a sewer were everywhere. In the distance there was a tune, maybe a song.

She became a corpse, a corpse all in the ground
And he became the cold clay and smothered her all around

A sudden moist warmth rose up from below, pushing away the coldness. Within seconds she felt on fire.

At the same time, Kit Farris experienced, again, the dream he had tried to forget, that had haunted him. It was the dream in which he cut the throat of his youngest daughter. Blood poured through his fingers, her eyes were wide with terror. A shimmering curtain of redness cocooned him.

As before, it was the cry of a name that woke him in a bath of sweat.

TWENTY FIVE

KIT FARRIS was quiet and peculiarly distant this morning. He was unsmiling, and somehow nervous, he had almost dropped a plate whilst standing at the sink earlier. His fingers trembled as he tried to place toast in the wire rack.

Sprog sat at one end of the table watching her father without comment. Bella also felt uneasy. She wished Pippa would soon be back.

Suddenly the telephone rang and Farris shot a wild glance to the side.

"It's only the phone, Dad," said Bella, trying to smile. "Do you want me to . . ."

"No," Farris retorted. "No. I'll get it."

He had been on the telephone earlier. She had been unable to overhear the conversation, but she guessed that it was the diocese office.

He slipped out into the hall like a sloping cat, closing the kitchen door as he went. Bella tried to listen to the conversation, but her father spoke softly and it was even harder with the door shut.

Farris recognized Mr Perkins' voice immediately. But the diocese secretary was not his usual self at all, speaking with a subdued voice instead of his sing-song titter.

"Mr Farris, I'll try to be brief. About my call to you earlier, explaining that I needed to give you information of a delicate nature. Mm, mm. I'm sorry I had to hang up, but one of our clerks suddenly came in, Miss Gerrard, whose been with the office a long time. I didn't want to speak in front of her, you'll understand why in a moment, I'm sure. This has all become rather distressing. Mm."

"Please go on, Mr Perkins. My girls are out of hearing range," said Farris. "I'll simply listen and comment if necessary."

"Good, good. I wish to discontinue discussing the history of the St Mary's site with your daughter, Pippa. Mm. I wanted to explain. Could you kindly invent some excuse, and tell her that I've become very busy?"

"What's the problem, Mr Perkins?"

"Somebody in London called me to explain that they had uncovered a curious fact about the Edric affair. I have a good contact down there, a historian. It's become like the secret service here suddenly, Mr Farris. Mm. The church had tried to suppress the story. It's about this Monk, this Edric fellow.

"Human remains—mainly bones—were discovered within the flint rubble walls of Edric's annexe workshop when traces of his work were being removed. Mm. They had also found a stone slab, which they had thought was a cutting block, stained with an ochre dye, but which they later realized was blood. Mm, blood. Bottles of it were found beside paint powder. Dried by now, of course. I need hardly dare suggest what was used to mix Master Edric's colours, but let's just say it was unlikely to have been water. There were many manuscripts. They contained spells, and descriptions of rituals, long forgotten stuff. There was also a collection of ceremonial knives."

Farris swallowed and murmured down the phone for Perkins to continue.

"I've found this all most upsetting. Mm. I don't want to frighten the young lady. A most unsuitable story. I have of course heard of such things before, but . . ."

"It's all right, Mr Perkins," said Farris in a sombre tone. "We're discovering some oddities of our own. Let me get in touch when I can. I can't talk . . . "

"Of course. The thing that bothers me most though was the remains."

Mr Perkins went quiet, Farris could hear his breathing.

He continued. "They were almost certainly those of children."

Farris heard the sound of a slammed door down the phone.

"Excuse me," said Perkins, "I must go now."

Farris replaced the receiver without giving any reply.

"Children . . . " he whispered.

He opened the kitchen door and stared at his two daughters. Something inside him, a hard edged logic, told him that this was all ridiculous. Why should folk tales unnerve him? He just needed a break, it was the place, wasn't it? Wasn't it?

Sprog had eaten her breakfast without saying a word. Her usual self had become displaced by something alien. Her eyes were knowing, yet they revealed nothing of what that knowledge might be. Farris crossed to the sink with a heavy sigh.

"What are we going to do today?" asked Bella, attempting to lighten the despondent air.

Farris made no reply. He started washing a few of the dishes, left over from the previous night.

"Daddy?" she tried him again.

He jerked his head round and glanced towards Sprog. Then he tried to smile at Bella in response.

"Sorry . . . sorry. I'm being thoughtful."

"Today, what are we going to do today?"

Sprog peered at him from over the edge of her toast.

"I . . . I . . . "

"Dad, what on earth's the matter?"

"Did, did I wake either of you at all last night?" he asked.

Bella frowned, "No, why?"

"I just wondered," he said dismissively, "I had a dream, that was all."

"Can you do my pony tail? Pippa usually does it for me."

The request caught him off guard, and then he pulled himself round. He wiped his hands on a tea towel and crossed to where Bella sat.

"Sometimes I think you're the most lady-like of my three imps."

"Of course," Bella agreed. "But today?"

He made a stronger, concerted effort, to snap back.

"I want to finish the frame clamp for the window. Pippa and Sarah should be here mid-morning, then we can put the thing into its place and see the effect."

He pulled her long hair into a tail and struggled with the tie. He continued to glance uneasily at Sprog.

"What about you, Sprog?" he asked, almost challenging her to reply.

Sprog still held her toast in front of her, little of it had been eaten.

"Sprog?" his voice became almost angry this time.

"I might play with Mister Damp," she said slowly, adding indignantly. "Then I might not."

"Mr who?" asked Farris, almost too abruptly.

"Oh, it's just a stupid name for one of her frogs," interrupted Bella. "You know Sprog's mind. Invisible friends."

"He's not invisible, stupid," snapped Sprog. She turned on Bella with fire in her eyes. "He's the biggest, King of them all and he's my friend."

"Then perhaps it's a toad," said Bella indignantly, "not a frog at all."

"He can be what he wants to be," said Sprog and

dropped the remains of her toast onto the table.

"Does it matter?" Farris completed the pony tail and swept back to the sink. "All little girls have 'special' companions, Bella, you know that. Remember when you had Mr Bunny?"

Bella preferred not to reply.

He rubbed his eyes and then splashed some water on to his face. He wondered what was wrong with him. Nightmares didn't usually get to him this way. For some reason he thought again about Mister Damp.

"Is Mr Damp magical?"

Sprog fell silent again.

"Sprog?"

"Yes."

Satisfied that the friend was imaginary, Farris stared out of the window, he thought he saw Bob Ford's head bob up above some hedgerows to the right of the front pathway. Perhaps he had come to do some gardening, although it looked like rain again.

"So we're not untouchables after all then, Mr Ford," he muttered with a smirk.

PIPPA SAT slouched in a pew. She had stopped her restless cantor up and down the aisle, her shoulders heaving with deeply taken theatrical sighs. The traces of annoyance had barely vanished, but at least she was sitting down, allowing a more philosophical attitude to settle in.

Above the scaffolding planks, the new central panel was held in place by Farris's concocted frame. The border sections had still to be inserted and these were filled in temporarily, with ordinary stippled glass.

In the central aisle stood Farris and Sarah. Farris stared up at the window, but Sarah was watching Pippa.

"I think it's excellent," said Sarah yet again. "The stain

is absolutely bang on, we just have to fire again, that's all."

Farris was clearly as irritated as Pippa.

"It is good. But it's not the firing, the thing's contaminated. Damn it. How did it get that wash in it? It's muddied the colour?"

"You were going to make it the proper window, weren't you?" Pippa said quietly.

Sarah eased along the pew and sat beside her. She raised a finger to her lips.

"We can do it again," said Farris. He turned towards Sarah. "The marks only came out in the firing. I knew the amber had been spoilt the moment we laid it down in the workroom." He added, "Never mind."

But Pippa knew very well that he minded.

"But how?" he said again, stamping his foot on the stone floor. Sarah flinched at the echo. "What caused it?"

He looked back at the window. It was unnoticeable at first. After a while it seemed to dominate the picture. A haze, as though granules were embedded within the glass, showed clearly. It spoiled the portrait of the boy.

Pippa looked miserable. The hardness in Farris melted. Things had got on top of him and it was little wonder. It was the place and the dreams, especially the dreams; and now there were horror stories. It had become a dark summer. Perhaps the girls should never have joined him here? Maybe they should even move out? *No*, he decided.

"Pippa, have you sorted out the small scenes from the paper I gave you?"

She looked up, "No. Not yet, I was going to look at them beside some verses, see if they helped."

"Well, when you've done it I'll commission you to complete them with me."

It did the trick, she almost shone in response.

"You can't always get things right first time," Sarah

said. "I had the head of a pottery sculpture fall off once, at an exhibition, too. I'll help you with the scenes."

All appeared to be well again.

"It's a pity it's so dull today, I'd have liked to have seen the effect with brighter light," said Sarah.

She suddenly stood up.

"Are your ladders still round the outside, below the window?"

"Yes," replied Farris, "why?"

"The halogen lamps, they've been fitted haven't they?"

"And used," he added.

They looked at each other for a moment.

"Go on, Dad," said Pippa, "shine them up on to the window so that we can see the effect of the colours, never mind the flaw."

"For you, anything."

A ladder leaned exactly beneath the newly placed window. He clambered up the aluminum rungs and carefully angled the hoods of the lamps so that they would cast a beam on to the glass.

He looked upwards, a wind was gathering grey clouds into a tumble of twisting, ever changing contours. Perhaps rain was coming.

"Don't like the look of that," he said to himself, and he re-adjusted the lamps away from direct rainfall.

As he went to clamber down again, he glimpsed a figure, back amongst the trees. Farris stared hard, lowering his eyelids to protect his eyes from the wind. He thought it was Bob Ford, and he was watching him, as if from a hiding place.

"What's the silly sod doing now?"

He felt a spot of rain and quickly continued to descend, almost missing his foothold several times in his haste. He'd talk to Bob Ford later.

Back inside the church, he stopped in the lobby and threw the newly installed switch. From within, he heard the sound of hands, clapping with applause.

"Come and see!" cried Sarah. "It's impressive."

He stood at the entrance for a moment. Pippa, Bella and Sarah were admiring the window. But Farris's attention was captured by something else, which they were unable to see. For a second the scene threw him completely, it was like a moment from an adventure film set in Egyptian tombs or another equally mysterious location.

A narrow beam of pale green light shone from the top of the window, across the church, to the head of the central aisle where the stone sarcophagus stood. There, the shaft collected into a small coloured pool, which perfectly reflected the stained glass insert on the lid.

"Hey, look, turn around, quick!" he cried.

Sarah turned and blinked.

"But . . . how?"

"That's amazing," cried Bella.

As they watched, the beam slowly faded, trickling away like the decay of bright sunlight when shadowed by cloud.

Farris hurried across to the tomb, the light had almost vanished. He arrived in time to see a final flicker of brilliance, as though a fire cracker burned inside. His mind raced, unable to understand what he had seen but totally engaged with the trick of it.

He looked up at the window.

Almost tripping over his feet, he tumbled down the aisle and squeezed himself along the pew to the scaffolding ladder. The others watched as he pulled himself up the rungs and on to the platform. He almost fell onto the boards.

He now had a better view of where the beam

had originated.

A glow shimmered around a small round orb, slightly larger than a marble. It was fixed into a circular section of glass, set at the pinnacle of the stone frame. Something cloudy, the colour of ink, twisted within.

"It came through here!" he called down. "It seems to act as a kind of lens. A focusing medium. It's clever."

Pippa moved out from the pew to the central aisle, to gain a better view.

She remembered noticing the glass orb when she had first climbed up there to look around. There was something about an eye too, she recalled.

"Inscription," she remembered, "there's an inscription isn't there?"

Farris searched the frame for letters.

"Here it is, *'Mine eye shall see my desire'*," he called back to her.

"It's from a psalm, I think," Sarah called back. "I used to sing it, believe it or not. Don't recall which psalm though. How odd."

Farris twisted round and looked down into the church. For a moment his head swam as if he had turned too quickly. Then he saw Sprog, crouched behind the sarcophagus. He caught his breath. His daughter was staring up at him, but she looked a different person. Her face was sour, displaying a bitter aspect he had never seen before.

She was clutching one of her jam jars as tightly as if it were a treasure.

The image of the jar catapulted up to him, for just a moment it was all that he saw. Suddenly, the reason for the contaminated window became clear. He recalled the moment when Sarah had first met Sprog. Sprog had been using his brushes and stains to design her heart. The same materials and tools which Pippa had used when she worked on the window.

He gave a long heart-felt sigh and brushed his hair away from his face. Now he knew the reason for the flaw.

As he backed down onto the first rung of the ladder, he paused and looked into the face of the portrait.

The features appeared to flex, as if viewed through a heat haze. For a moment he thought another kind of activity was beginning to break out.

"What? Another face . . . ?"

He shook his head.

"No. I'm tired," he said to himself.

He continued down the ladder to the apparent safety of solid ground.

TWENTY SIX

"SHALL I stay for a while?"

Sarah Prestwood looked kindly into Farris' face. He closed his eyes with gratitude at the suggestion.

Pippa linked her arm through her father's.

"I'll try and make some sense out of the border scenes, for the window, this afternoon."

Bella smiled, as easy going as ever. Sprog still remained distant, like a nervous cat uncertain of its territory.

They returned to the house, where Sarah made tea. Farris wanted to work on the remaining frames.

"We'll stay in the workshop, shall we?" Sarah asked, as she brought in a tray. "We can mull over Pippa's outstanding puzzles."

Pippa agreed.

"Keep an eye on Sprog, too."

"Going to get my pencils," said Sprog with a huff. She marched off to the bedroom.

Farris pushed the door closed after her.

"Sarah," he hissed, "all of you. Listen a moment. Sprog's in a very strange mood."

"We can see that," Pippa muttered.

"She's just got out of the wrong side of the bed again," offered Bella. "It's nothing serious."

"Nevertheless . . ." Farris began. "Just keep an extra eye on her. Another thing." He glanced at Sarah. He held Pippa's hand. "I'm sorry Pippa, but I think I know what the problem was with the window."

He took another deep breath.

"Clean the brushes thoroughly and chuck out all the stains on my worktable. You used the brushes and colours that Sprog was using, remember she had that jam jar with the pond water or whatever it was?"

Pippa groaned, realizing that he was right.

"Surely, it shouldn't have affected it that badly though?" Sarah asked him.

He thought for a moment, the effect had been peculiar.

"Perhaps, perhaps not, but it's about the best I can come up with now. It sounds more plausible than some other things that are happening around here."

They heard the door handle turn and Sprog returned. She still looked odd. A bunch of pencils was held tightly in her fist.

"Come on, sweetheart," said Sarah, bending down towards Sprog. "Cheer up. I see you're wearing that lovely pendant which Pippa made you."

Sarah reached out to adjust the string. Her hand froze mid-way, her face creasing into bewildered concern.

Farris noticed her grimace.

"What is it?" He crouched down beside her.

Sprog showed no emotion.

"It'll be all right," muttered Sarah. "Come on, love, I think you're wearing this too tight. You're getting a rash or something."

She lifted the necklace from around Sprog's neck, and then gently tilted her head to one side.

"There's a red mark around her neck," said Pippa, noticing it for the first time too.

Farris lifted Sprog's chin. He was rougher than Sarah. A red line, as if it were the burn from a cord or string, stretched wide across her throat.

"Is this sore?" Sarah asked.

Sprog moved her head slowly from side to side, the edges of her mouth remaining downturned.

Sarah felt the mark with her fingers, stretching the skin

to see if there was a lesion. Sprog gave no response.

"The necklace was rubbing. It looks okay though," she announced, loosening a knot in the cord.

Farris jerked upright as though he'd just received a shock.

"Kit?" asked Sarah, catching his reaction.

He felt unable to speak. The memory of the dreams had rushed into his head, arriving there with a fullness that pushed away everything else.

"It's only a red mark," said Sarah. "She'll live."

She saw him swallow, his eyelids flickered as though surfacing from a deep sleep.

"Yes. Yes."

He went over to the doorway and paused with his hand on the edge of the door.

"I must get on." It was all that he said.

"Don't worry." Sarah nodded at him. "I can stay until six. Get on with your work."

He was about to reply, but shuffled slowly instead and leaving, pulled the door shut behind him.

TWENTY SEVEN

SARAH AND Pippa sat at the workshop table, pondering over various pieces of paper. Pippa laid out her father's sketches of the existing sections of window border. Beside this was a list of what she thought they meant. She also compiled a list of the biblical quotes that she had found scattered throughout the church.

Sprog sat beside the window, watching the drizzle weave down the pane, the summer had suddenly shed tears. Bella read quietly, occasionally glancing up to check on things.

Sarah studied the various sheets. Finally, she threw her hands up.

"Well, some of this is explained now, isn't it, thanks to the lamps and that beam trick? I'm damned if I can sort all of it out, though."

Pippa picked up a drawing of the small window section. She had thought that it was a picture of some kind of ritual bath originally. The copy was exact, but now it appeared that the 'bath' might be the sarcophagus in the church, and the diagonal line, the beam that they had seen from the upper section of the window.

She looked at Sarah.

"You think that . . . ?"

Sarah made a *who knows?* face.

"But what's this other figure doing pouring something into the sarcophagus?"

"Ritual washing? Like running a bath?" Pippa laughed at this idea.

"Well," Sarah continued, "you never know, after all, it was a common practice—still is, of course. Perhaps light is supposed to enter through that crystal thing at a certain time and do something to the water?"

"Yes, I follow. What about the other window scenes?"

"Well," she sniffed, "you may be right about the Lazarus picture, or at least it is someone rising from the tomb. I agree that this is a Well of some kind, but other than that I'm stumped. I just don't know about the others. Someone here is supposed to be carrying a pail or bucket . What have we got on sayings?"

Pippa unfolded her list.

Sprog, who sat nearby, shifted on her stool and looked over with mild curiosity.

"Above the panel, where that beam came from, it said: *'Mine eye shall see my desire'*. I went round and checked on the others: *'those that look out of the windows be darkened,' 'light of moon be as light of sun'*. There are several others in obscure places, there may be more. *'Spring up O well'* and *'shall bathe himself in water.'* That's all I've got. I've written the references, got them from the Bible Concordance and I've looked them up but they're no help. I think they were put in as a tease."

"Or as coded instructions for posterity!" said Sarah. "You are quite a little antiquarian aren't you?"

Pippa felt complimented but concerned and looked at the drawing again.

"Bathe—maybe that is what it is. *Bathe*, bits about a well?"

Sarah scratched her head. Her eyes were searching for something, trying to recall a comment she had heard. She remembered her mother's story about Edric, how he was taken from the tomb and thrown into a well.

"We're going to have to sleep on this," she announced.

"I've got that postcard to have a good look at, too," said Pippa. "The one Dad got at the cathedral."

FARRIS CROUCHED at the top of the scaffolding, feeling a stiffness in his joints. He had been working on a neighbouring window, prising out the remaining section of glass for matching. Extra lamps were rigged onto the scaffolding bars, his eyes sought out every corner as he worked.

He never heard the door of the church open. It was the echo of the twist of a heel which made him look over his shoulder. He looked down through the ladders. The ring of hard heels on the stone floor followed, sounding like the slip of loose roof tiles. He peered down the aisle to see who it was. Bob Ford stood there, po-faced and grim. He was looking up at the window.

Slowly, Farris pulled himself to his feet.

"Ah, Mr Ford," he said with a sarcastic twist in his voice. "I thought we'd lost you. Where's your dog?"

Bob Ford jutted out his chin.

"Bitch won't come here, won't sniff at the door even, specially not now."

Farris grabbed a cloth and wiped his hands.

"Mr Perkins gave me summat for you,' Bob Ford went on, "I've got it here."

Farris signaled to him to wait and then turned to make his way back down the ladder, carefully, rung by rung.

The two men met eye to eye, at ground level. Farris felt uncomfortable, especially now that he could clearly see the look on Bob Ford's face. It was more than just disapproving, there was an element of disdain there.

Bob Ford held out a brown envelope. Farris thought that either it had been badly re-sealed, or he had opened it.

"From the new chap."

Farris took the envelope.

"Like I said. There's some stuff there what he turned up, thought it might be of interest to you, bearin' in mind what you're doin' here. He didn't want to phone."

"Thank you," Farris replied curtly.

Bob Ford remained still, as though expecting Farris to say something more. When he did not, he stood back and looked up at the window again.

"Good work," said Bob Ford. "I saw you put it in, was watchin' you from the outside."

"I thought it was you. It's only a dummy, there's something wrong with the stain."

"Mr Perkins turned up a sketch of the face, don't know if it's original, probably not, but it'll do. Seems like you've got it spot on though doesn't it?"

"Eh?" Farris didn't follow the point he was making, then Bob Ford gestured towards the envelope with his hand.

Farris ripped it open, and leafed through the sheets.

There was a long letter and photocopies of something written by hand. There was also a photocopy of a drawing, it was faded, but the image was plain enough for Farris to tell that it was the head of a youth.

"Original was drawn from life, Mr Farris," said Bob Ford.

"Sam Stone?" asked Farris. The face had an awful familiarity.

Bob Ford made an empty, dry laugh.

"I never thought, when they got you in to do place up, tha' you'd put the poor little bastard back there."

Bob Ford nodded in the direction of the window.

"I use' to play here when a lad, loads of us did. But the play was dare stuff. Who'd stay in the house back there, or the church, the longest. You know, before runnin' out in case Chauncey Barrow or his conjured thing came after you. Then we heard the pitiful cries and couldn't go in there no more. My gran' told that her mother knew who it was, and that it were a warnin' to someone. None of us wanted to hear it, case it were meant for us. The boy was never found, Mr Farris. Barrow must have done away with him."

"*Conjured thing*?" asked Farris.

Bob Ford looked up with a twitch.

"You said conjured thing?" repeated Farris.

"The one what did some of the drawin' for these damned windows, of course. Nobody ever saw him, or it, properly. Black thing from hell we heard tell, had always been here. Re-cycles itself, dies and is reborn. Has special tricks, that's why Barrow rose him up again. Thing may have been 'ere since creation for all I know. Since creation. . ."

Farris felt dizzy, he had more than enough.

"Good afternoon Mr Ford," he firmly declared.

Bob Ford stared at Farris with eyes of iron, and then turned on his heels and walked towards the lobby entrance. As he opened the door he twisted round.

"Mr Farris?"

"Yes."

"You know tha' when you've gone, after tha' young Mr Perkins has paid out good Christian wages to you, the window will be broken, accidentally of course. It's nothin' personal. Don't put too much fine labour into it. I know you're good, Mr Farris, a real craftsman, but . . . you're wasting your'n damn time."

Bob Ford left before Farris could answer.

Farris became angry, wondering if he had just been threatened. He threw his apron down. Slowly, he stepped back, along the aisle and looked up at the window. It was becoming dark outside and impossible to see his work in detail. The portrait looked distorted from below, and he had to move his head to try and gain a better view. The light was playing tricks. It did seem different.

He looked down at the photocopy of the sketch and then back at the window again. There was an uncanny similarity, there was no mistaking it. He thought that he had drawn something neutral—featureless. But now . . .

He shook his head and pulled his hands out in front of him.

"Kit Farris," he said to himself, "you're going stark raving bloody mad. Do you hear me? Go back and offer to take that woman out tonight, do something different before your head explodes."

He walked towards the lobby and switched the lights off without looking back once, afraid of what else he might imagine.

TWENTY EIGHT

AN UNSEASONABLE chill bit the late evening air. A small fire of logs and peat had been started by Farris in the bedroom fireplace, before he left for Sarah Prestwood's.

A marvelous, seductive atmosphere, had entered the Grange, bringing with it an uncommon sense of well-being. Pippa stretched herself out in a huge wing chair, in front of the fire. The chair was old, spotted with woolly balls of stuffing that protruded from gashes in the upholstery. She felt very comfortable. The flickering of the fire made dancing figures, whilst casting warm-coloured waves across the walls and ceiling.

Even Sprog seemed contented at last. She sat cross-legged in the corner, playing with something in front of her. Bella lay on her stomach, across a mattress. She had been trying to read earlier, and had now fallen asleep.

Pippa felt pleased that her father had gone out with Sarah. He had hesitated when the time to go arrived, but she assured him that they would all be fine; he eventually left with an uncertain look in his eye.

The old notebook that they had found in the schoolroom, lay face down in Pippa's lap. She had played with the edges of the end pages, trying to prise them apart, and having failed, allowed her head to loll to one side of the wing.

Suddenly, there was a rush of wind within the chimney breast. The flames of the fire leapt more wildly in the grate.

Through half-closed eyes, thin red fingers flexed and waved to her, from within the yellows and oranges.

Bella remained asleep.

From out of a feathery trance, Pippa heard her name called.

"Pippa, Pippa. I've left it outside."

The voice sounded some way off, small and pleading.

"Pippa, Pippa. Please, can I go?"

Pippa slowly opened her eyes, a ray of light spread before her, a small figure somewhere within.

"Pippa?"

This time the voice was inside her head. The face, framed by boyish dark brown hair, stared hard. The eyes, insistent black points. She knew it was Sprog.

"My pendant, I've left it outside. I won't be long."

Pippa made a series of comforting swallows and closed her eyes again. She didn't want to open them properly.

"Hurry up though, it's late."

Sprog brushed past the side of the chair. The wind in the chimney sang Pippa a lullaby, rocking her back inside her heart.

INNOCENT VOICES, angel notes, rose and fell. It was a psalm, perfectly sung. Pippa was back in the schoolroom. But it was difficult to see, everything was draped in black folds as if ragged curtains hung from the ceiling. She weaved in and out of the dark spots, brushing through veils as if keenly searching for something or someone. A cry emerged from out of the singing: the recurring cry, but now very emphatic.

The shape of a person twisted and turned, adopting one attitude first and then another.

The cry became urgent. Its plea filled her ears and she vaguely became aware of shaking her head angrily from side to side, as if trying to throw off something which clung.

A message, desperate and insistent.

'I've been waiting here to warn you, all this time, for so long, why didn't you listen?'

Pippa felt her head hit the side of the chair, the fire glowed through sticky eyelashes.

'Come back to me. You must open your eyes.'

She felt herself sink into the depth of the chair. The cry continued, becoming shrill and anxious.

'The method is in the window, it is there that the danger lies. Why don't you listen? Do I have to show you it all, it is so, so awful? Must you know the pain?'

Pippa murmured. The schoolroom spun around her, spinning faster until suddenly, it stopped. She found herself standing before a shadow.

For a moment, she hesitated.

She reached out, and as though snapping a curtain back, pulled the darkness away.

A dreadful scream filled her ears; it was her own.

Thunder echoed in the distance.

The boy within the shadow lifted his head for her to see. A blue light flashed within the bright blade of the knife as it was swept across his throat. A deep red fountain of liquid life gushed, grotesquely exaggerated, into her view.

FARRIS GAVE a moan of horror.

He braked as a sudden red-brown wash coated the entire windscreen. It had appeared from nowhere, as though thrown from a bucket. For a moment he was unable to see the road ahead. The camper van swerved for several feet, planing on the surface of the water and then skidded to a halt on the verge. With a single sweep, the windscreen wiper cleared an arc.

A blue fork weaved across the sky, away above the fields, and a silver sheet sparkled within the beam of his headlights. The rain beat hard upon the camper van, sounding like sleet on a tin roof.

He gulped desperately like a fish fighting for air.

"What . . . ? What did I hit?"

He sat perfectly still.

Hands shaking, he unbuckled his seat belt and opened the door. The rain beat his hair into a flat mop within seconds, but he didn't care. He could only stand and stare at the windscreen. The wipers and the rain dissolved the colour, even as he listened to his heart-beat.

He reached out a nervous finger and wiped the screen, he brought his finger closer to his face, unable to believe what it could be.

"My God," he whispered, "oh my God, surely not. But how?"

The rain washed the blood away as he stared.

He turned and reached into the glove compartment for a torch. He walked back along the road, shining the beam in all directions, anxiously looking for any sign of a body: animal or human. He wondered if it might have been a bird, blinded by the downpour. But there had been too much blood for it to have been anything so small. The wash across his windscreen had been like a wave.

He stood still for a moment, allowing the rain to trickle down his face in a cold caress. Fissures of silver fell around him.

"I hit a bird," he told himself, quietly. "I must have done. Just calm down. I hit a bird. A bird. A big bird, goddamnit. It was a good evening, now get back to the girls."

Something of guilt, just a splinter, began to burrow into him.

He walked back to the camper van and gave the torch one last cast about the ground. There was only the thrash of the rain on the road to see, as puddles sparkled from the flash of summer lightning.

He turned to climb into the camper van and froze.

An imprint or stain, had formed on the windscreen, an outline of a face, indistinct yet recognizable in glistening red. After the wiper had made several more passes, the rain washed the image clean away.

"Sprog?" His mouth felt swollen, starched.

The headlights suddenly dimmed.

TWENTY NINE

SPROG WALKED from the bedroom quietly. She never stopped to get a coat, and left the house through the back door from the workshop, closing the door as she went.

The slap of the rain across her face, and the sudden flash of light above, caused her to pause briefly. But only long enough to gain her bearing and to consider the easiest route across to the church.

She had to stop at the sundial first.

Sprog crossed the lawn with an easy amble, not caring that her clothes were beginning to stick to her body. The rain was coming down so hard now, that it stung her face. She paused before the corner of the garden, where the hedgerow almost hid the sundial.

For a moment she tried to remember why she was out here. Hadn't she left her pendant somewhere? Was that it? The voice had told her to look in the church.

A shaft of silver from above, lit the lawn in a gleaming green. The hedges moved, the wind was rising steadily now. She wondered if someone was coming.

She gave an inviting smile.

Someone *was* coming, whistled there by the wind.

Here he came, her summer companion.

A cold quiver passed through her: a glamour was deceiving her.

"Hallo," she said as he approached, a shuffling shambling damp form.

THEIR WALK to the church, was slow. The thing that held Sprog's hand moved with difficulty across the mud. It had paused at each of the rain filled ditches, as if attracted to the water. Sprog heard a gentle sucking sound each time, followed by a restless shifting as though it might be reforming or renewing itself.

Between the crash of each thunderclap, Sprog gained a moment's escape from the glamour. She thought she saw something squashed and folded into a terrible huddle, beside her. Its eyes burned deep within the crease of a fold. The skin was mottled and grey, dead and wet. The mouth was small and round, with thick pursed lips, poised to deliver an awful kiss. She felt very afraid. But suddenly, a further shimmer of blue-light showed her that she need not worry. Her companion was, after all, the one who had shown her so many secret things since her arrival: Mister Damp.

The companion, who could cast the glamour over her so easily and deceive, who could make her believe that it was anything it chose, held her hand in his. She thought at first that her fingers might slip from his hold, they felt so wet, but gradually she became aware of a sudden strength within his tightening grip.

Suddenly, she slipped away into a soft cloud. She was aware of being inside the church, standing at the head of the aisle.

The shape appeared to grow.

"What do you want, Mister Damp?" she asked, as it turned towards her.

Sprog watched the blackness stretch up and over her as it moved forward. Almost without realizing how she had got there, she knew that she was now on her back, staring up at the church ceiling. Had she been placed in some kind of container? She remembered moving something for Mister Damp. He had pointed and she had known exactly what she must do. Now, a darkness was coming, slowly, slowly.

Eventually, she saw nothing at all as though a door in a dark room had been tightly shut.

The blackness clung to her. She felt it pass through her wet clothes, seeping into her skin. She tasted it on her lips. There was an oldness about it, but it was older than just decay. It was even older than time.

From another place, there came a great roar. A green eye crackled with power, just above her face. There was a stirring, like the flow of soft mud, beside her.

KIT FARRIS lifted his hands to his face. He pushed his fingers into his eyes. A weight of grief descended, the like of which he had never felt before, not even at Isabel's death.

He tried again to start the engine, but it merely coughed and shuddered as though its heart had given up.

He stared through the windscreen and saw visions of his work. Faces, outlines on glass, all rushed at him. The colours—the stains and enamels—ran into one another, becoming an ugly mixture. The figures began to droop, their faces lengthening into skull-face masks, the lead curling at the edges and allowing the panes to crack and fall.

He remembered the face in the window at St Mary's and howled.

THIRTY

A WHITE FISSURE split the night sky, transforming the room into daylight for a moment. A clap of thunder, louder than before, followed. Pippa and Bella awoke at the same moment. Without exchanging a single word, they knew that something was very wrong. They ran to the window in time to see another jag of lightning spit down through the clump of trees, into the place where the church stood.

For a moment a glow ran into the night sky and then died.

"Sprog?" asked Bella, turning to Pippa, her arms spread wide in anticipation of a reply.

Pippa looked blankly and rushed across to where Sprog had been sitting earlier. She had been very preoccupied with something in the corner.

Her hand shot to her mouth, when she saw the remains of the dead animal with which Sprog had been playing, so peacefully. She thought it looked like a rat. A kitchen knife lay beside it, it had been skinned and part of its entrails had been laid out neatly.

Bella felt confused.

Pippa gave a groan; she remembered Sprog's voice from the trance-like nap, asking if she could go out to get something. For a moment she was not sure whether she had dreamt it or not.

"Search the house!" Pippa snapped. "I think she's outside, somewhere, but let's make sure first."

"Out in this?" Bella was shocked.

"Don't talk—move!"

They tore through the house like a pair of raiders,

screaming and calling. They pulled back bed covers, in case she had slipped away to sleep, and searched rooms they'd never been in before. There was no sign of her.

They came together in the hallway at the bottom of the stairs.

Pippa was shaking with anger at herself. She had always been so sensible, so serious and grown-up, and now she had given her little sister permission to go out in a raging storm. She wished for a moment that she could fold into something small, and vanish.

Bella reached out and held her sister's hand, trying to pull Pippa's tear-filled eyes back to hers.

"Where, now?"

"I've an idea, that she's in the church. She'd lost her pendant you see, the one . . . the one I made her."

"Come on," said Bella, pulling Pippa behind her.

THE RAIN lashed their faces as severely as a cat o' nine tails. They might have been moving through the eye of the storm, which had singled them out for attention.

As they crossed the lawn, they never noticed that the far corner of the garden had been blown into a strange funnel shaped clearing, or that the sundial glowed with a pale, dead light, more sinister than the greyest moonshine.

Ahead of them the ground heaved, thick with mud, greedily pulling their feet back into the earth with each step they took. Within the clump of trees, they saw the embers of the remains of scorched branches. Tiny spots of yellow light that alternately faded and grew with the wind. The rain had put a fire out, and Pippa muttered grateful thanks to someone that the church was not ablaze. Then it crossed her mind that, perhaps, that was the best thing that could possibly have happened to it.

They hurled themselves over the top of the boundary fence. Bella fell awkwardly into the soft turf. She cried out.

"What is it?" Pippa yelled, forging ahead.

"My knee, I've done something to my knee!"

Bella pulled a face and managed to straighten up.

"Go on, I'll manage," she called.

Pippa returned and offered Bella her shoulder to lean on. Together, they continued their way through the trees. Bella gritted her teeth and limped.

The tree trunks became frightening obstacles. At each flash of lightning, the thick shapes stood proud against brightly lit blue bark. The girls stopped and exchanged fearful glances. They joined hands and pressed on, Bella now managing to hobble without the support of Pippa's shoulder.

A further shimmer of light showed them that they were near the side of the church, below the new window. A black patch appeared to fall from the window, dropping down the wall like a draped veil. It was a powdery burn.

"It hit the window!" cried Pippa, "I don't believe it!"

"It hasn't broken the glass though, has it?"

It was difficult to tell.

They hurried on, breaking hands now, so that Pippa could go ahead.

The door was already ajar when she reached the porch. Pippa brushed the hair away from her face. She threw the switches to light the church, but only a pale amber squeezed out from the edge of the inner door. She tried the new control, which operated the halogen lamps, she was surprised to hear a faint buzz from the switch, and an unnatural brightness swelled the gloom.

She was now joined by Bella, who was clearly in pain.

They pushed the door which yawned wide without creaking.

The white walls had become transformed into a mottled beige which seemed to ripple, as though alive. The unevenness of the stone was cast into grey pits, which reminded Pippa of pores. The scaffolding threw strong black angles, like a giant web across to where they stood. From the outside, a single halogen lamp lit up the window in strong commanding colours, a mosaic of colour shining on to their anxious, peering faces. The window had been undamaged, except for the smoke mark, which almost settled into the pattern as if it had been intended, and another's hand had put the final touch to the piece.

Pippa cried out.

"Sprog! Sprog! Where are you?"

Bella joined her, the two voices seemingly competing with one another as they searched the place. Pippa scuttled along the front pews, like a chased mouse, looking beneath the seats with eyes that threatened to bulge from her head. Bella dragged her leg behind her as she checked the rear.

"Sprog!" cried Pippa again, this time finding it more difficult not to choke on tears.

Bella's sudden scream brought her up sharp. She twisted about to face the rear of the church. Bella was stood beside the sarcophagus, pointing up at the window.

"Look!"

Pippa followed the line of her arm.

"No, please no, don't let it be ... " she hardly heard her own words.

"It is, isn't it?" screamed Bella.

Pippa moved slowly down the central aisle, her eyes riveted to the face of the figure. It was still only an image, a painting, but it had changed. The lips were parted now, that was the feature which clinched it, the gap toothed grin grotesquely imitated in stained glass.

"Just like the dream . . ." Pippa murmured.

Bella became a small and hunted thing. She dropped down beside the sarcophagus, crumpled lines on her face trembled. She could no longer feel any pain.

"What, what did you say Pippa, what?"

"Sam Stone was trying to tell me. Signs, omens, dreams. Chauncey Barrow took his soul and put it in the window so that he would be his, captured. Then he murdered him. And now, after all these years the thing has come full circle. His vile assistant has returned."

Bella reached out to push herself up, her hand found something small with a sharp edge, attached to a cord.

"Pippa!" her hand closed around the pendant.

Pippa looked back, Bella held it high for her to see.

"It was here, beside the sarcophagus!"

"It would have to be," Pippa yelled, "she's in here—that would make sense, Bella, believe me, Sprog's inside the tomb!"

Bella dragged herself to her feet and tried to shift the lid, it was a pathetic and pointless endeavour.

Pippa joined her and together they attempted to lift the thing by its edge. They glanced up at the window. Outside, the storm continued to rage as if all the anger of the world had been summoned there tonight. The figure was lit with snatches of brighter colour, as splashes of light poured on to the glass. The terrible run of red, which crawled downwards from the neck of the figure, had increased. Now it glistened and dripped out from the frame and down on to the wall, tracing red river tributaries.

Pippa stared at the sarcophagus, her fists clenched.

"Pippa! What are you doing?"

"Thinking, thinking, thinking."

She walked around the sarcophagus.

"Sometimes, just sometimes there were levers, catches that opened these things."

She felt beneath the rim of the lid but found nothing. She pushed sections which might have been panels. Suddenly, she noticed the stone projection at the end, which seemed to be in the shape of a face. As she stepped back, she thought that she saw something crawling across the lid. Bella saw it too, and fell back with a cry. The scheme of fleur de lys appeared to be slowly shifting, as if they were real leaves, rustled by a wind. Within the pattern, faces began to peer out at her. The features were tiny and squashed like a crumpled ball, and reminded her of deformed toads. But the eyes betrayed warning as if they might be guardians, set to watch over the tomb. She blinked hard, for a sudden moment they seemed to become a sheet of wriggling maggots. Then they vanished. She heard a voice inside her head.

'Don't be afraid.'

Pippa glanced back at the stone face.

Quickly, she reached out and grasped it with her entire hand. She pulled the image at first, and then noticed some give. She turned it.

Something sharp, like needle teeth, bit into her palm. She winced from the pain, but held on. A low grating, like the crawl of old rusty cogs against wheels, echoed into the building. She snatched her hand away as the lid of the sarcophagus slowly pulled to one side. An odour, dark and heavy wafted from the opening.

Bella gripped the edge, peering anxiously into the tomb, as below, a black shadow parted, allowing the beige and orange glow within the church, to fill the interior.

"Sprog!" Bella shouted excitedly.

Sprog lay at the bottom, eyes open and staring upwards.

The slow parting of the lid seemed like an eternity. Pippa leaned into the tomb, she reached down and tried to pat her sister's face.

"Sprog, can you hear me? Sprog?"

There was no response. Pippa wondered if she was dead.

The lid ground to a halt and Pippa clambered inside. There was very little weight to her sister, and it was an easy task to lift her out.

"What's wrong with her?" Bella's face was screwed into an uncomprehending expression.

"I don't know," replied Pippa quietly.

They laid Sprog out on the floor of the church, Pippa kept glancing upwards to the window. "She's so pale, why are her eyes open?"

"Sprog!" Pippa leaned across and shouted into her face. "Sprog!"

There was still no response. Her chest gently rose and fell, but scarcely any breath left her body. The pupils of her eyes became black pin specks.

"Is she going to die?" asked Bella, her eyes now moist pools.

"No!" Pippa snapped, "No!"

"Her neck—Pippa, look at her neck!"

She hadn't seen it.

The red mark across her throat looked dark and angry. Even as they stared at it, the colour appeared to deepen.

"Pippa!" Bella was almost beside herself now. "What are we going to do?"

Pippa shook Sprog hard, it was like shaking a rag doll.

She stood up, her mind searching back through all that had happened to her, what she had seen and heard, desperate for a scrap of detail which might help.

"Omens!" cried Bella, "you said you were warned,

dreams and things. If we know what happened then perhaps we can reverse it somehow?"

Pippa recalled the voice which had visited her during the storm—*the 'method' was told in the stained glass.*

Suddenly, she knew exactly what to do.

Behind them, a door crashed open. The wail of the wind rose.

Pippa span round. Her father stood in the doorway, his hair was straggled across his oil marked face, which looked haggard and tired. He fell against the frame.

THIRTY ONE

FARRIS CRADLED Sprog in his arms, as he gently rocked from side to side. He moaned softly in a long monotone to the rhythm of his sway. His eyes felt like bleached orbs and he hardly noticed the dreadful slush and mud that covered his daughter..

Sprog had begun to imitate her counterpart in the window. Blood was congealing into a thick line around her neck, and the stained glass figure oozed a terrible pattern.

Sprog still breathed, but barely, her face expressionless and open as though in a kind of trance.

For several minutes Pippa could get no sense from her father, she held him by the shoulder and shook him. Bella stood by, watching, not daring to believe what was happening, hoping that it all might be part of a bad dream.

"Dad!" Pippa shook him again.

She turned and ran to the sarcophagus, and looked about the floor for the pendant. It was still there. The heart was like a blot against the red of the stone. She picked it up and rushed back to her father.

Again she shook Farris, harder, and held the pendant in front of his face.

"It's a chance it might work—but you've got to do it, it's too tricky for me!"

His eyes couldn't see her. She took a deep breath, and pulling her hand back for a second, slapped him hard across the cheek. His face registered instant shock.

"Listen to me! Put the pendant in the window, set it within the figure!"

He stared at her as though she were a stranger. "To break the evil something good has to be put into the image, put this into the figure! Remember the dove at the cathedral! The monk and the apprentice are one and the same, do you hear me!"

She pushed the pendant towards him. He couldn't understand her.

"Please, please, do it. I know what I'm saying. Be careful not to break the window, put the heart into the figure—trust me. I can't explain, not now—Sprog's going to die if you don't!"

Something sparked alive inside him. He carefully let Sprog's head rest back on to the floor.

His hands were wet and sticky with her blood. He sprang to his feet and made for the scaffolding. As he climbed the rungs of the ladder, the beat of the rain on the glass reverberated within his head. At the top of the scaffolding, he came face to face with the image. It was unsettling, the colours smearing with a murky wash.

His cutter and pliers lay with other tools on his work box. He picked up the cutter and began to etch a starting point in the chest area of the figure.

Below, Bella saw Sprog flinch as if something had pricked her.

Pippa held her hands in front of her body, the fingers tightly knitted whilst Bella stroked Sprog's forehead. Back within the shadows came a familiar voice.

"She needs attention. Come down, hurry."

Pippa looked round. There was a short person standing just by the lobby door. Sarah Prestwood stepped out of the dark, her face unsettlingly calm and serene.

"Can you hear me—now's not the time to be listening to folk tales, this child needs help."

Farris had just finished a section large enough to insert the pendant, he stumbled with surprise, almost dropping the cutter.

"Let me take her," Sarah insisted, "I knew something was wrong and came out after you." She stepped towards the place where Sprog lay. "We've got to hurry."

Farris froze. He turned back to the window. Through the hole which he had cut, he heard a drop in the wind. This wasn't right.

A silence fell.

Only the sound of the rain could be heard.

Pippa could see Sarah clearly now, then it hit her like a sudden blow. *Sarah Prestwood was as dry as a bone*.

She turned on the woman and snarled, "You've got to be joking, bastard!" She yelled up to her father, "Don't listen to her! It's not Sarah! Do you hear me? It's not Sarah!"

The woman's lip curled, her eyes narrowed to slits, as she raised her arm as though making a command.

A boom, huge and sudden like a cannon shot, echoed around the church as the door flew open. A shaft of blue light poured in through the entrance. They heard a roar like a great wave. Pippa saw it coming through the open doorway.

The pathway gravel outside, heaved suddenly into a hump, the height of a man. For a moment it looked alive, and then it rushed forward spitting stone as if it were grapeshot.

The girls screamed as it crashed through the entrance and scattered about them. Pieces of shingle cut into their arms and legs, their faces became red pits.

The woman stood, untouched, within the midst.

"The pendant!" Pippa screamed. "Dad! For God's sake!"

Suddenly, the scaffolding began to shudder. Farris reached out and grabbed a bar, leaning forward he wedged the pendant into the opening. Almost instantly, the window began to glow. Something powerful radiated from inside the pendant itself and it spread outwards, through the colours like a comforting heat.

From below, came a wailing cry of anger, of one who had been cheated.

The scream hailed an abrupt silence which caused them all to stiffen. The remaining loose gravel scuttled to rest across the stone floor and then there was nothing more. Not even the sound of the wind or the rain.

The woman could have been a melting waxwork. The features drooped instantly, and the arms and legs appeared to lengthen. After a moment the head and the torso began to sag and fold into themselves. The body turning soft—like clay. At first it changed to a beige and then a green, glistening like an enormous squashed toad.

Sprog blinked and whispered.

"Mr Damp . . . is that you?"

The children watched, mesmerized.

Farris cried out, "No!"

The thing was still below with them. He looked about, searching for something to throw and saw the window again. The face had changed once more, and he knew whose portrait it was.

He gasped. A female voice he had not heard in over three years, filled his head.

'Look up, Kit.'

He looked to the point of the arch. It was where the glass orb had been fixed, 'the eye'. He remembered the effect with the beam, how it had shone down on to the sarcophagus. But now a dark twist, like a leech, swam within it.

Quickly, he unclamped a short bar from the corner of the scaffolding tower.

With teeth gritted tight, he rammed the end of the bar into the orb.

Something black, like a jet of ink, spurted from the glass.

A death rattle roar shook the air as an awful sigh, a final breath, echoed around the walls and descended through the earth to a place he dared not imagine.

It had been like pulling a plug.

He turned and stared down.

Twisting strings of amber and green smoke remained, like will o' the wisps, hanging silently above the floor. There was a faint smell of burning.

Pippa and Bella sat huddled together beside Sprog, who was now moving. She had just sat up and was stretching her arms as if they had cramp. Then she stretched her head back. The mark around her neck had gone. There was only smooth untainted skin.

The glow had now left the stained glass pane, and the face had returned to the image he had first drawn. He reached out and withdrew the pendant. He looked at it closely for a minute and placed it in his trouser pocket. He stood quietly, letting the moment clear his thoughts.

He lifted the bar and began to smash the entire window out of the concrete frame.

THE NIGHT was clear, like a summer's night should be, the stars a bright roof, which lit their way to the camper van which was parked close by. The storm had been taken from the face of the earth.

They spent the rest of the night together in the back of the camper van. Farris locked the windows and doors and watched over his children, not daring to close his eyes.

THIRTY TWO

BY THE time all of the three children had awoken, Sprog being the last to rub the sleep from heavy eyes, Kit Farris had already been up for more than an hour.

Pippa suddenly recalled the terrible events of last night. For Sprog it was like waking from a long and deep summer dream.

Bella had scrambled to the front of the camper van and was watching through the windscreen. She stared intently into the tree clump where the church stood, listening to the faint sound of tinkling glass. Pippa heard it too.

"He's locked us in," said Bella in a calm, matter-of-fact voice. "It will be okay, he won't be long."

Farris was setting his ladder below the last two remaining windows along the west wall. His face was nicked from flying glass, but it was also hard set and determined. He climbed quickly to a spot below one of the windows, and swung his iron bar into the centre. A kaleidoscope of shards of colour showered outwards.

It felt satisfying.

He was not content until he had run the bar around the edge of the concrete, ensuring that every bit had been removed. Then, with a full smile across his face he began to climb down again.

He felt someone's eyes watching him. He paused on the ladder half way, and glanced over his shoulder. Bob Ford was looking up at him, his dog crouched low beside.

"Morning Bob," he said.

"Mornin'."

"Going to be a fine day I think. Just finishing some business, don't mind me."

"I shan't," said Bob Ford.

"Up early, eh? Do you have a moment to help? There's a stone box inside that's got to come out too. I've a couple of hefty mallets."

"Wha' about Mr Perkins?"

"We had a really dreadful storm last night, didn't we Bob, shame about all of this."

Bob Ford grinned.

"Stretchin' it a bit. Tha's true though, didn' I see it all myself too."

He spat on his hands and began to take off his jacket, as he walked towards the church entrance.

MATTERS BECAME much clearer later that morning, when Sprog showed them the well, where she had collected her jam jars of water. Pippa shuddered as she realized what must have been put into the window. Farris had looked at the border drawings again, it was easy to see how it all came together. The 'soul taking' appeared to have a set ritual, the subject laid in well water. 'Light of moon be as light of sun' had provided a clue too, only last night had no need to wait for moonshine to catch the glass orb and beam into the sarcophagus. The sudden brightness of lightning had channeled everything into the church. Unwittingly, Sprog had provided her own magical water, and—very nearly—something else.

Back at the Grange, the brooding atmosphere seemed to have lifted. Pippa immediately went upstairs to the schoolroom where the spirit of Sam Stone had waited for over a hundred agonising years to warn them.

"He's gone," said Pippa, as her father joined her.

"And so will we be," he said. "Get your things."

Reaching into his pocket he removed the pendant. He held it in his palm for a moment. He was going to ask her about it, but instead he said nothing and handed it to her.

"It was made with love too. That's why it worked."

Pippa wondered if he had guessed that she had put a pinch of her mother's ashes into the pendant.

He heard a noise outside, and went to look out of the window.

A fraught looking Mr Perkins was making his way across the garden towards the house, followed closely by Sarah Prestwood.

He met her at the door. Sarah Prestwood walked towards him, her face a neutral mask.

"Hist whist," she said.

Kit Farris held his breath.

EPILOGUE

Dear Mr Farris,

It is now nine months since we last met and I must apologise for the delay in writing to you. However, in the light of the extraordinary affair with St Mary's I just thought you might be interested to learn of a couple of addenda (if I may describe them as such). Whether or not you pass these on to the children will of course be your decision.

Last month, the borough surveyor insisted that the newly discovered well in the garden of the Grange be excavated and examined. The local council were worried about it for a number of reasons; safety, and the fact that tests revealed an extremely strange and toxic substance down there. There is the possibility of all kinds of health hazards and so on.

The well was drained and capped off, though it has, till now, remained dry. An initial investigation revealed a large underground chamber at the bottom, separate from the water area. I don't know if this was the reason for the unusual circular steps. As you may appreciate, this is rare in a reservoir of this age, arguably earlier than medieval. An archaeologist visited the site and we found something rather grim.

The gases from the water must have some sort of preserving quality about them, that's one theory at any rate. We discovered human remains in the chamber that are very old indeed, a hundred or even two hundred years old. One set, hardly human, are impossible to date at all. All that was left were bones, but some skin had dried in places. I must tell you that the archaeologist nearly had a fit when he happened upon it.

There were three bodies. What must have been an elderly person, according to one opinion, had his arms fixed tightly around the body of a younger. They were frozen in some sort of horrible embrace. Locals have been quick to speculate on this. Mr Ford was naive enough to ask if the child's throat had been cut! How could we tell? I'm afraid I don't doubt that it may have been.

The third figure was very strange. It was found positioned a little away from them, fixed there as if watching for some reason. It was crouched on its haunches like a frog. The remains of an old piece of vellum was discovered close by (this was a type of paper once used by the monastery). It was a partially completed drawing, apparently of the awful coupling. I laid off work for several days, I felt so upset.

The archdeacon is saying prayers, and the child's bones will be laid to rest in consecrated ground.

Finally, you may be interested to know that enquiries as to who might have destroyed the Chauncey Barrow window at the Cathedral have now been dropped. The police have put it down to vandalism. As you know, I still have my suspicions.

As before, I'm sorry that you were unable to complete the contract, but I think I now realise a little better what the problems were. I saw Mrs Prestwood recently, who talked of you and her daughter. I gather you have retired from stained glass and considering pottery, possibly a joint venture I understand? I'm glad that some good came out of this business.

I was going to enclose a print I was given for your youngest child, of a character in The Wind and The Willows, a charming book, an excellent print too. Uncle Monty, a distant uncle of mine sent it with some books, recently. Mrs Prestwood informed me, however, that your family no longer has anything at all to do with toads, frogs or any other form of pond life. Probably a good job too.

I remain, yours,

E.Perkins
Diocese Assistant Secretary

Laurence Staig's fiction includes the award winning collection of short stories *Dark Toys and Consumer Goods*. He is also the author of *Technofear, The Glimpses, Digital Vampires, The Network, Carnival of the Dead* and the new collection *Told at Dusk, Remembered at Dawn*, forthcoming from The Brooligan Press. He co-authored the first ever published study of the Italian Western and created the much used description of the genre "The Opera of Violence"

THE SEBASTIAN BECKER NOVELS
Stephen Gallagher

*Chancery lunatics were people of wealth or property whose fortunes were at
risk from their madness. Those deemed unfit to manage their affairs had
them taken over by lawyers of the Crown, known as the Masters of
Lunacy. It was Sebastian's employer, the Lord Chancellor's Visitor, who
would decide their fate. Though the office was intended to be a benevolent
one, many saw him as an enemy to be outwitted or deceived, even to the
extent of concealing criminal insanity.*

*It was for such cases that the Visitor had engaged Sebastian. His job was
to seek out the cunning dissembler, the dangerous madman whose resources
might otherwise make him untouchable. Rank and the social order gave
such people protection. A former British police detective and one-time
Pinkerton man, Sebastian had been engaged to work 'off the books' in
exposing their misdeeds. His modest salary was paid out of the
department's budget. He remained a shadowy figure, an investigator with
no public profile.*

THE KINGDOM OF BONES
After prizefighter-turned-stage manager Tom Sayers is wrongly
accused in the slayings of pauper children, he disappears into a
twilight world of music halls and temporary boxing booths.
While Sayers pursues the elusive actress Louise Porter, the tire-
less Detective Inspector Sebastian Becker pursues him. This
brilliantly macabre mystery begins in the lively parks of Phila-
delphia in 1903, then winds its way from England's provincial
playhouses and London's mighty Lyceum Theatre to the high
society of a transforming American South—and the alleyways,
back stages, and houses of ill repute in between.

*"Vividly set in England and America during the booming industrial era
of the late 19th and early 20th centuries, this stylish thriller conjures a
perfect demon to symbolize the age and its appetites"*
—New York Times

THE BEDLAM DETECTIVE

...finds Becker serving as Special Investigator to the Masters of Lunacy in the case of a man whose travellers' tales of dinosaurs and monsters are matched by a series of slaughters on his private estate. An inventor and industrialist made rich by his weapons patents, Sir Owain Lancaster is haunted by the tragic outcome of an ill-judged Amazon expedition in which his entire party was killed. When local women are found slain on his land, he claims that the same dark Lost-World forces have followed him home.

"A rare literary masterpiece for the lovers of historical crime fiction."
—MysteryTribune

THE AUTHENTIC WILLIAM JAMES

As the Special Investigator to the Lord Chancellor's Visitor in Lunacy, Sebastian Becker delivers justice to those dangerous madmen whose fortunes might otherwise place them above the law. But in William James he faces a different challenge; to prove a man sane, so that he may hang. Did the reluctant showman really burn down a crowded pavilion with the audience inside? And if not, why is this British sideshow cowboy so determined to shoulder the blame?

"It's a blinding novel... the acerbic wit, the brilliant dialogue—the sheer spot-on elegance of the writing: the plot turns, the pin sharp beats. Always authoritative and convincing, never showy. Magnificently realized characters in a living breathing world . . . Absolutely stunning"
—Stephen Volk
(Ghostwatch, Gothic, Afterlife)

"Gallagher gives Sebastian Becker another puzzle worthy of his quirky sleuth's acumen in this outstanding third pre-WW1 mystery"
—Publishers Weekly starred review

NIGHTMARE, WITH ANGEL

After rescuing Marianne Cadogan from an incoming tide on a
lonely and forgotten part of Britain's coast, ex-con Ryan
O'Donnell is cornered into helping her escape a supposedly
abusive father to reach the safe custody of her mother. Too
late, he finds himself compromised, the subject of a trans-
European manhunt while he struggles to deliver the child and
prove his motives pure. The deeper in he gets, the more
trapped he will become

THE BOAT HOUSE

A dark love story, and a disturbing tale of a divided soul. In the
days leading to the fall of the Soviet empire, a young woman
with a deadly secret slips unnoticed into the West. And when
Alina Petrovna first appears in Three Oaks Bay it's clear that
her frail, luminous beauty is likely to cause some ripples in the
surface calm of the peaceful resort town. For Pete McCarthy,
the boatyard worker who gives her shelter, she's an enigma. A
complex, well-meaning young woman with a difficult past.
Someone whose mystery deepens as the season gets under way,
and the deaths by drowning begin...

Printed in Great Britain
by Amazon